THERE WAS NO ONE ALONG THE SHORE.

But as he reached the middle of the beach, a pale flash of movement caught Reever's eye. When he realized what he was seeing, he froze in disbelief.

Tory had risen and thrown off her nightshirt. As naked as the moonlight itself, she walked with measured steps away from the edge of the cliff, turned as gracefully as a dancer and walked back toward the brink.

No! Stop! The desperate cry went no farther than Reever's mind. It was too late. Tory had reached the brink and sprung up and outward. Arms spread wide, body perfectly arched, she floated through the air as though she were truly the swan from which her dive had taken its name. She entered the midnight lake, and the water was barely disturbed.

Reever could have called out, could have stopped Tory, but he was frozen in the moment when she had dived into the lake with a grace and beauty that had literally taken his breath—and his heart.

ELIZABETH LOWELL

Too Hot to Handle

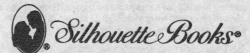

Silhouette Books®

Published by Silhouette Books New York

America's Publisher of Contemporary Romance

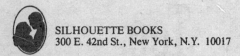

SILHOUETTE BOOKS
300 E. 42nd St., New York, N.Y. 10017

TOO HOT TO HANDLE

ISBN: 0-373-48249-3

Published Silhouette Books 1986, 1992

All the characters in this book have no existence outside the imagination of the author and have no relation whatsoever to anyone bearing the same name or names. They are not even distantly inspired by any individual known or unknown to the author, and all incidents are pure invention.

®: Trademark used under license and registered in the United States Patent and Trademark Office and in other countries.

Printed in the U.S.A.

One

Tory Wells hung on to her battered luggage with both hands. She felt as though the earth had been ripped from beneath her feet. It wasn't the earth being ripped, however. It was the letter that she had brought with her from Ethan Reever's cousin, a letter promising her employment on the Sundance Ranch.

"But I was told that—" she began, her voice low, urgent.

"You were told wrong," Ethan Reever interrupted ruthlessly, dropping the shredded, unread letter into an exquisitely woven Pima basket that held other paper debris. He gave the slender young blonde in front of him a hard glance. "There's no swimming pool on the Sundance so there's no need for a 'swimming counselor.'" His lips thinned in disgust over the last two words. "And unlike my dear cousin Payton, I have no use for bleached blondes who can't do two licks of work without whining about their nails."

"My hair isn't bleached, my nails are short and the day I whine you can fire me," retorted Tory, setting her luggage down with a thump.

Reever laughed. The sound was as hard as the large hands that slapped the desk in an impatient movement as he came to his feet. "Honey, I haven't hired you, and I'm not going to. I need you like a sidewinder needs ice skates."

Tory stared in silence at the man looming behind a desk that was as scarred as her luggage. Reever was nothing like his cousin, Payton Sundance. Payton's hair was straight and sandy, he was clean shaven, his eyes were a sparkling blue and his body was as thin as it was tall. Reever's hair was thick, blue-black and shaggy. So was his mustache. His blunt, angular face showed a shadow of beard, even though it was barely eleven o'clock. His eyes were the color of winter rain and were emphasized by heavy black eyebrows. He had the long, powerful bone structure of a natural athlete and the muscular development to go with it. He was at least six foot three—a dark, intimidating presence watching her with eyes that gave away nothing.

Reever's intense masculinity would have made Tory nervous if she hadn't been so desperate for the job. She was accustomed to being around men with flawless bodies, swimmers and divers whose lives were dedicated to physical perfection, yet never had she met a man whose very presence could send frissons of heat searching through her. Reever threatened her in ways that she couldn't describe. But even more than he threatened her, he fascinated her. She found herself wondering what it would be like to be held in those powerful arms. Did that beautifully shaped mouth ever smile gently, and were his hands capable of tenderness as well as strength?

Tory shook herself mentally, wondering if she had lost her mind. Reever was very unlike his cousin. She could well believe Payton's warning about Reever's "devil temper." Payton was charming, kind and known for his generosity throughout the Southern California amateur athletic community. Tory doubted that anyone would use the adjectives generous, charming or kind to describe Ethan Reever.

The thought didn't make Tory back down. She had spent her life working with male coaches who could most politely be described as "difficult." Besides, she had to have the Sundance job whether Reever was devil incarnate or angel in disguise. At the moment she had exactly two dollars and sixty-three cents to her name. She couldn't afford a bus trip back to town, much less a cab—not that either bus or cab was available, even if she had money. The Sundance Ranch was in the wild country of northern Arizona, a place where the roads were empty and the land was full of sunlight and silence.

"Mr. Reever," Tory said carefully, trying to show neither her desperation nor her fear, much less the very feminine curiosity that he aroused in her. She had learned early in life than any sign of weakness would be used against her.

"Reever," he said, his voice harsh. "Just plain Reever. You're not in the city anymore, Miss Victoria Wells."

"No kidding?" shot back Tory. Her glance went pointedly around the office, where a collection of spurs was tacked to the wall and a half-braided horsehair rope waited in one corner to be completed. "Call me Tory, Reever," she said, smiling. "Everybody does."

His eyes narrowed. Tory decided that all the books were wrong. The devil's eyes were gray, not black. She took a deep breath and tried again to get past Reever's hard exterior. Somewhere inside that man was something more than harshness and the glacial cold of his eyes. She knew that with an instinct so deep that she didn't question it.

"Mr. Sundance assured me that there would be work for me here," Tory said honestly. "I came a long way at my own expense on that assurance. If the Sundance Retreat isn't open yet, there must be something else I could do on the ranch until the retreat opens."

Reever stood silently for a moment, giving Tory the same kind of thorough, cataloging glance that she had given to him a moment earlier. Tory knew exactly what he would see. She had short blond hair streaked by the Southern California sun, green eyes that were too light to be called emerald and five feet seven inches of tan body conditioned by a lifetime of swimming and diving.

If Reever was hoping to make Tory uncomfortable with his stare, she had a surprise for him. She was used to being stared at while wearing a good deal less than beige cotton slacks and a T-shirt proclaiming "Be Kind to Endangered Species—Adopt a Mermaid." Competition swimsuits were designed to be a second skin, and they achieved that purpose with admirable thoroughness, especially when wet. As Tory stood on a diving platform high above a pool, poised for her second dive, the spectators knew just about everything there was to know about her physically.

Yet standing still for Reever's slow scrutiny became more difficult for Tory with each passing second. When he looked at her, it was as though his hands were moving over her body while his fingertips learned every feminine curve and hollow. The thought both shocked and intrigued her, making her breath shorten and her eyes darken as the pupils expanded with sensual curiosity. Deep inside Tory a gentle heat began to uncurl, making her mouth soften in unconscious invitation. She was too inexperienced to realize what was happening to her; she only knew that the longer she watched Reever, the more she became curious about him as a man.

"Please," Tory said, her voice husky. "If you had read the letter before you tore it up, you'd know that I'm a very hard worker."

Reever hadn't finished his leisurely appraisal of Tory's body. When he finally did, his mouth turned down and his voice shifted into a sardonic drawl that could have etched steel.

"No, thanks," he said. "I like my playmates small, stacked and sexy. You flunk on all three counts."

For a moment Tory was too stunned to respond. Her breath came in with a rushing sound as her temper flared. "I wasn't offering to—" she began angrily.

"The hell you weren't," interrupted Reever, his eyes as contemptuous as his tone. "You were begging for it."

Tory flushed, then went very pale. "Go to the devil, Ethan Reever," she said, trembling.

"Didn't Payton tell you, honey? I *am* the devil."

Tory looked at Reever and wished suddenly, violently, that she had spent her years learning karate rather than the gentle art of diving. Without a word she picked up her luggage, turned her back on the devil's cruel smile and walked out of the room. Before she had gone three steps, she heard the desk chair creak as it once again took Reever's formidable weight. The sound of the big leather ledger sliding across the desk was loud in the silence. She didn't need to look over her shoulder to know that she had already been wiped from Reever's mind as completely as though she had never stood in front of him and pleaded for a job.

Without hesitating, Tory walked through the living room, opened the front door and pulled it shut behind her, using her foot. She would have slammed the door until the house shook but had no wish to call attention to herself again. Just the thought of facing Reever's contempt brought a sweeping humiliation that was as great as her anger. She would crawl on her hands and knees all nineteen miles back to town before she suffered his contemptuous appraisal again.

Although the ranch house was thousands of feet above the desert floor, the June day was hot enough to bring a mist of perspiration to Tory's face as she stood on the porch and looked at the long, dusty ranch road that eventually led to a narrow county road and from there to Massacre Creek, the only town within ninety miles of the Sundance Ranch.

Tory knew from experience that the most exciting thing about Massacre Creek was the name. The sign outside the town had proudly proclaimed Population 401, but unless they were counting the litter of fat puppies that she had seen chasing flies and each other in front of the Sunup Café, Tory couldn't imagine where Massacre Creek's citizens were. After the relentless concentration of people in coastal Southern California, northern Arizona's empty reaches seemed alien and . . . oddly inviting.

At the moment, though, Tory could have done with a little less scenery and a lot more cheap public transportation. Abruptly she shifted her duffel bag over one shoulder, took a better grasp of the cracked, abrasive handle of her suitcase and stepped off the porch onto the dusty gravel drive. If she wanted to be in town before dark, there was no time to waste on wishful thinking.

Tory pushed aside the thought that there was almost no chance that she would be able to walk nineteen miles before sundown. Without luggage she would have done well enough. There had been some days when she had driven herself to swim nearly that many miles under the sarcastic goading of her coach. She hadn't been carrying a suitcase, however.

And then there was her knee.

Slowly Tory walked over the treacherous gravel, alert to each movement of stone beneath her right foot. She didn't want to think about the knee injury that had finally resulted in surgery three weeks ago. She didn't want to think about the doctor's final frightening words, words that had sent her rushing to Arizona with no more than a few dollars and Payton Sundance's letter in her purse. She had come back from an injury before. She would do it again. All she needed was the time to heal and the money to survive until she could take up the physical demands of her swim club scholarship again.

Tory was relieved when the gravel gave way to dirt road, but the relief was premature. She soon discovered that the rutted, washboard surface of the road was as tricky to walk on as the gravel had been. Trial and error taught her that the best walking was on the very edge of the road, where tires had passed often enough to make a flat trail but not often enough to leave ruts and ripples in the dirt. Her luggage tended to hang up on roadside bushes, but there weren't many rocks to bruise her feet through the worn soles of her shoes. Where her little toes had poked through the canvas, pebbles worked into the holes and from there to her tender feet.

At first Tory stopped and emptied her shoe every time a pebble got inside. She soon gave that up. She was spending more time hopping around on one foot and dumping out the other shoe than she was walking. So she just kept going until the first pebble was joined by a second and then a third, or until her arms and shoulders sent threatening messages to her brain. Then she would stop, dump her luggage in the dirt, stretch and empty her shoes.

The carefully rationed rest stops were far too short, but Tory knew that she didn't dare extend them. She really didn't want to be walking through the countryside after dark. Her best chance of a safe ride into town was to catch the mail carrier somewhere along the county road. She wished that she had listened more closely to the woman's friendly chatter as she had delivered Tory—and a generous supply of junk mail—right to the Sundance Ranch's front door. Had the woman said that she made a loop that led back to town after a circuit of ranch roads, or had she said that she went out the south end of town and came in the north?

If it were the latter, there was no hope of getting a ride back into town. Nor did Tory want to take her chances on hitching a ride with a stranger. Living in cosmopolitan Southern California had taught her not to trust strangers. If she kept walking, she would get to town eventually. She had no such assurance if she hitchhiked.

By the time the Sundance Ranch's dirt road met the two-lane blacktop of the county road, Tory was bathed in sweat and aching in every limb. She hoped that the road's dark, even surface would ease the throb in her right knee. She had no such hope for the burning of her blistered palms. Swimming might have strengthened her body, but it had done nothing to toughen her hands or feet.

With a stifled groan Tory remembered the mail carrier's words to the effect that it was five miles to the Sundance ranch house from the county road. She couldn't believe it. She had to have walked more than five miles. It couldn't be fourteen more miles to town.

"Stop whining," she muttered to herself. "Whining takes energy. Think about something pleasant—like drowning that arrogant son of Satan in the deep end of a pool."

Stretching, smiling, Tory thought of having Reever gasping and begging for mercy at her hands. It was a fantasy she had often had about her coaches in the past when they pushed her beyond what she thought she could endure. But each time she was pushed she had learned that she *could* endure. Not only that, she had learned that she could strengthen and improve until workouts that once would have left her gasping became nothing more than invigorating exercise. Until their bodies were conditioned, though, she and her teammates had spent many hours planning complicated and satisfying vengeance on their various coaches.

But when Tory thought of revenge on Reever, the picture of him apologizing for not giving her a job kept going out of focus. In its place came a sudden, searing image of him bending down to her and his large, hard hands cupping her face gently as he whispered against her lips that now that he had found her, he would never let her go. The image shocked her. It made her realize that in a few minutes Reever had had more impact on her than other men in the same amount of years. She had never been in love, never wanted to be in love—but now she wondered what it would be like to love and be loved by Ethan Reever.

"Sidewinders will be ice-skating in Reever's birthplace before that happens," Tory informed herself sarcastically, feeling a flush climb up her face. "He couldn't have been clearer that he thought your attractions . . . weren't. Face it. His eyesight is as sharp as his tongue."

Small, stacked and sexy. You flunk on all three counts.

Tory wished that she could disagree with his assessment, but she could not. She was tall, gently rounded, and in all considered herself about as sexy as an ironing board. Although her hair was a shiny, many-hued blond, it was also a short, softly curling cap. The first rule of being a sexy blond was that your hair had to be a long, ravishing, silky mass slithering down between your shoulder blades. The second rule of a sexy blonde was that your chest had to be a double handful for any man, and your heart-shaped bottom had to swing like a bell when you walked. The third rule was that a sexy blonde was always ready, willing and able to trip a man and beat him to the floor.

"Face it, Tory. Even if you could trip that devil, you wouldn't know what to do next."

The thought shook Tory. She had grown up watching the sudden passions and equally sudden separations of her teammates. The pressures of competition and endless, grinding workouts were often relieved in brief, volatile affairs. She had seen that usually it was the girl who was hurt. It was the girl who paid the price emotionally, competitively and in terms of her reputation. There were exceptions, of course—boys whose competitive edge was dulled by a failed love affair or girls who changed partners as casually and frequently as they changed swimsuits—but those exceptions were very few.

Tory had decided before puberty that the dubious rewards of "love" really weren't worth the costs. Life had taught her that men simply weren't capable of caring. Her father hadn't even noticed her when he was still living with her mother, no matter how many medals Tory had won in competitive swimming. After the divorce her father had simply vanished, sending nothing to his daughter, not even a card at Christmas. Nor had her stepfather been much better. He had begrudged every penny spent on Tory, pointing out to her many times that her father was a selfish jerk who had never sent a dime on child support and never would. Her mother had rarely interceded; she was too grateful to find a man to support her. Later Tory had realized that she had been born three months after her mother's first marriage, when her mother had been barely seventeen.

When Tory's stepfather had been transferred to Wisconsin, she had stayed in California and moved into an apartment with three other girls from the swim club. Within days she had a job working from 8:00 p.m. to 2:00 a.m., five days a week, at a nearby fast-food restaurant. Three months later she was promoted to cook when the boss found her filling in for a man who was more interested in partying than in working.

The hours were awful, the work was hard and the money was barely enough to survive on. Yet Tory wouldn't have traded one minute of it for life with her stepfather. Her boss agreed to schedule her around her swim meets and school, and in return Tory worked even harder. When the doctor had told her to take a minimum of three months off from diving, it had been a great temptation for her to stay in Mission Viejo and work double shifts and save money.

In the end Tory had reluctantly decided against it. The doctor had been determined that she remove herself from the "narrow, unnatural, short-lived, hothouse atmosphere of Olympic athletics." He had flatly told her that she was to get out, all the way out, to see something more of the world than an Olympic swimming pool and then to decide if going back to diving was worth the risk of a permanent crippling injury.

Hastily Tory bent and picked up her luggage again. She didn't want to think about the doctor. He was wrong. He had to be wrong. Her knee would heal again and be stronger than ever. She was sure of it. It would be like everything else in her life had been: if she just worked hard enough, long enough, and depended only on herself, she could do anything. Anything at all. Including walk nineteen miles through a hot Arizona afternoon and find a place to stay in a town so small that it hand-lettered changes on the population sign. Then she had to earn enough to pay for the room and to buy a bus ticket back to California.

"One thing at a time," Tory said aloud, stilling the rush of her thoughts. "It's like a competition. You can't worry about any dive but the one in front of you or you'll fall apart. So first you walk to town. Then you can worry about the rest, one thing at a time. Just like diving.''

As Tory thought of standing on tiptoe on a platform more than thirty feet above the aquamarine perfection of an Olympic pool, she unconsciously licked her lips. At the moment, even pool water would have tasted good, chlorine and all. And to arc up and out, to turn over and over before entering the water's stillness, to have her tired body embraced and supported by the cool water...ah, that would be heaven itself.

Head down, her duffel bag slung across her back and her blistered hand grasping the broken handle of her suitcase, Tory set off down the two-lane county road, limping slightly. As far as she could see, she was the only thing moving beneath the incredible blue of the sky. She was relieved to be so alone. She had been in cities for too long to relish the idea of meeting a stranger on that desolate road.

Reever rode along the southeast boundary of the ranch, checking the range. It had been a good winter, a wet winter. Snow had lain thickly in the steep-sided mountain valleys and had melted slowly on the slopes, providing continuous natural irrigation for the meadows. Grass and wildflowers grew in profusion, brushing his stirrups, for Reever hadn't permitted this part of the ranch to be grazed for five years. He had wanted just one part of the Sundance to look as it had in his great-grandfather's time.

Sundance, Jawbone and Wolf creeks were brimming with bright water, as were the sloughs where birds gathered in wheeling clouds to raise their young. Despite the raucous birds, it was Wolf Creek itself that drew Reever's eye. It had been a long time since he had tasted fresh trout. Although the water was still quite cold with the runoff of barely melted snow, the fish should be shaking off their winter torpor and gliding through the green pools in search of the season's first insect hatch. Cold, clean water and winter-hungry trout—a fisherman's dream.

Reever's mouth turned down as he admitted that, even if he managed to tempt one of the wily trout on to a hook, it was unlikely that Cookie would turn the fish into an edible dinner. Cookie had been restless lately, which meant that one day soon the hands would show up for dinner only to find that there wasn't any. Then the men would comb out the bunkhouse or the barn and find Cookie, drunk beyond sobering. He would stay that way for two days, two weeks, whatever it took to temporarily appease the demons within. Lately it seemed as if Cookie's demons came more often and stayed longer.

Swearing under his breath, Reever told himself that he really had to find another cook. He'd been telling himself that for two years. He would have done it, too, but finding a cook who didn't mind the Sundance's isolation wasn't easy. With another muttered curse, Reever pulled the buckskin to a stop at the crest of a bank overlooking a series of pools joined by brilliant white ribbons of tumbling water.

One of the pools was directly in the sun. The color of the water was a green so luminous that it seemed to quiver with life. He had seen nothing to compare with that green—until this morning when a girl as slender and supple as a streamside willow had watched him with sensual curiosity darkening her big eyes.

"Payton Sundance, you charming, blue-eyed son of a bitch, if you ever send me another of your cast-off playmates, I'll peel your soft city hide and nail it to the barn."

The horse twitched a black-tipped ear at the harsh sound of Reever's voice. Stamping uneasily, the animal registered its awareness of the sudden tension sweeping its rider.

"For God's sake, she couldn't have been more than sixteen," Reever continued in disgust. "City nymph with hungry green eyes and a body like a cat's. Sleek. Graceful. Made my hands itch just to look at her. And when she looked back at me..."

Reever shifted in the saddle as his body responded to the memory of that delicate face tilted slightly to the side, eyes wide and luminous and as sensually curious as the lips that had parted with a tiny rush of sound. The temptation to go right over the desk and slide his tongue into that sweet mouth had been so strong that it had first surprised and then angered Reever. As he had told Tory, he didn't need a pretty, useless female. He already had two of them, and he had been supporting them since he was sixteen. When he found a woman, she would be just that—a woman, not a girl. She would be quiet, enduring, and she would love the Sundance as much as he did.

He had been a long time looking for a woman like that.

With a snort and another stamp of its hoof, the buckskin settled into a lazy, three-legged stance. The horse was accustomed to its rider's peculiarities. One of them was to sit and look over the ranch while the wind curled around him, bringing the rich scents of a fertile land uncluttered by man.

After a final curse Reever forced himself to look away from the Wolf's radiant green pools. He congratulated himself for throwing Tory out on her tempting little fanny. The last thing he needed was a paternity suit or an arrest for contributing to the delinquency of a minor. Besides, once he had her, he would lose interest, she would pout and things around the ranch would go to hell in a hand basket. No matter how mature they thought they were, girls that young always believed at some level that sex with a man meant love everlasting. Yes, he definitely was well rid of little Miss

Victoria Wells. Payton could damn well find another home for his former toy.

But God in heaven, what a walk she had. Smooth. Feline. Hot.

A thrust of desire went through Reever like raw lightning, making every muscle in his body suddenly tighten. Before he knew it, he was full, aching, ready. The speed and the force of his arousal surprised him. At thirty-three he was too old to go off like a teenager. But there it was, hard against his jeans, silently demanding release.

With a sound of disgust at his own unruly sex, Reever lifted the reins and urged the buckskin down the faint trail. Cold water climbed almost up to the animal's black hocks, and stones grumbled beneath steel-shod hooves as the horse plunged through the icy creek, sending up sheets of spray on either side. Drops of water more brilliant than diamonds flashed in the air, shattering sunlight into a thousand tiny rainbows. Reever laughed suddenly, a different laugh than he had used on Tory earlier. This laugh was vital, rich, alive, a sound of pure sensual pleasure.

"You do love crossing that creek, don't you, Blackjack?" asked Reever, giving the horse's neck an affectionate slap. "Your mammy must have been part beaver."

The horse snorted and pranced, tugging at the bit, plainly asking for the freedom to run.

"Sorry, boy," said Reever dryly. "At the moment I'm in no shape to oblige you."

With a disgruntled swish of its black tail, the horse settled into a gliding, ground-eating single-foot that was part walk, part pace, as smooth as water, fast and much easier on its rider than a gallop. Before long Reever reached the top of a fold of land that overlooked the southeastern part of Sundance Ranch. Without waiting for a command, Blackjack slowed and then stopped, for this was one of Reever's favorite places. The country stretched away before him to the far blue horizon, a land unencumbered by man but for the dark ribbon of the county road winding between green meadows.

A tiny movement at the corner of his vision caught Reever's attention. The motion would have been overlooked by most people, but he was accustomed to the land. He knew the difference between the pale flash of a hawk stooping on its prey and the languid movement of a white-faced cow cropping lush grass. What had caught his attention was neither hawk nor cow nor startled rabbit. It was someone walking along the county road. The figure looked no bigger than Reever's thumb at this distance, but he had no doubt that it was two-legged rather than four.

"Well, Blackjack, someone's truck must have broken down. We'd better see if they need help."

Even as Reever reined the horse in the new direction, he saw a bright red car slowing. He expected the car to stop, take on a passenger and pull out again. When the car stopped but no one got in or out, Reever was surprised. When the car raced off, made a U-turn, then raced past the pedestrian, made another U-turn and stopped suddenly again, Reever reached into his saddlebags for the binoculars he always carried.

"Looks like the Metlock car," he muttered, focusing the glasses. "Wonder who Billy's hurrahing today. Damn that kid. Eighteen years old and more coyote than man. Somebody should have taught him manners by—"

Reever's words broke off. With a single vicious curse he spurred Blackjack into a dead run.

Two

―

Tory heard the car screech to a stop for the second time and tried to still the frantic beating of her heart.

Three of them are just kids, she told herself firmly. *Not even old enough to drive.* Then helplessly, *God, but they grow them big out here!*

"C'mon, baby," called the redhead, hanging out the window of the dusty Ford. "We don't bite. Well, not where it shows anyways, if you get what I mean."

That witticism brought a chorus of raucous cheers and whistles from the boys in the back seat.

Tory ignored them. She'd heard a lot worse the first time they went by. The driver in particular had yelled the kind of filth that she had rarely heard, even during the overnight shift at the restaurant when drunks had come in to drink coffee and grab at the waitresses. She had learned to ignore the obscenities; any other attitude only encouraged them.

Acting as though she were alone, Tory kept walking. She had already refused the driver's leering offer of a ride with a cheerful "Thanks, but I like walking." There was nothing more she could do except look straight ahead and keep on walking. Or run. She wouldn't do that yet, but she had decided that the instant a car door opened she was going to throw her luggage over the barbwire fence that ran alongside the road, and then go through the fence herself.

Tory hoped that wouldn't be necessary. Except for the driver, the carload of boys was more obnoxious than really threatening. She hoped that they would be satisfied with baiting and insulting her and would tire of the sport quickly when she refused to answer. Above all she hoped that if she went through the fence they wouldn't follow her. She had little doubt that she could outrun the rude, rawboned teenagers as long as her knee held out. That was what really worried her. Her knee. It was already tender from the long walk.

The bright red car stopped a few feet in front of Tory. The driver's door popped open. Tory didn't stop to argue or plead or find out how many boys were getting out. She threw her luggage over the fence and followed it, tearing her T-shirt and her skin on the wicked barbs. She didn't even notice the pain. She began to run, sprinting for fifty yards before she risked a look over her shoulder. Only the driver was still following her. The rest of the boys were through the fence but were using their breath on catcalls and laughter rather than running.

After that single quick look, Tory ran on at a headlong pace, breathing harshly, tearingly, her heart beating so fast that it frightened her. Suddenly she heard the rolling thunder of a horse running flat out over the land. From the corner of her eye, she caught a blur of movement as Ethan

Reever flashed past her, bent low over the neck of a huge, hard-running horse.

The driver saw Reever, too. The big teenager turned and raced back toward the fence with more speed than he had shown in chasing Tory. She sank to the ground and tried to catch her breath. All at once she began crying and shaking. She held on to herself and fought for control, trying to force herself to breathe deeply, evenly, until the adrenaline-induced hysteria had passed.

Reever shook out a loop of the long rope that he always carried strapped to his saddle. Billy was close now and getting closer with each one of Blackjack's long-legged strides. Reever coolly waited until Billy was almost to the fence, almost free. Then Reever's arm shot out and a loop of rope settled sweetly around the teenager's broad shoulders. The instant the rope tightened, Blackjack stopped running and sat right down on his hocks, bracing himself as though Billy were a mean half-ton steer needing to be thrown.

Billy's feet flew up and he sat down so hard that his hat jumped off his head. As soon as he had caught his breath, he struggled to his feet. Blackjack surged backward, yanking Billy flat again. With a light touch on the reins, Reever spun Blackjack and trotted toward Tory. Billy bumped along behind like an oversize sack of potatoes.

"You all right?" Reever asked, stopping near Tory.

She looked up into the pale blaze of his eyes and felt almost sorry for the overgrown boy on the end of the rope. She nodded, knowing that her voice would shake if she tried to answer.

The buckskin spun on its heels and backed suddenly, yanking Billy flat once more. Reever dismounted in an easy, flowing motion and went to stand over the big teenager. He waited until Billy met his eyes.

"It's a good thing your daddy's dead, boy," said Reever flatly. "He'd have peeled you clean as a willow switch for a stunt like this. I've got a mind to do it myself."

Billy couldn't meet Reever's eyes any longer. The boy's glance fell on Tory. He saw her pale, dirt-streaked face and the hints of blood where barbwire had ripped through her T-shirt. He looked away quickly.

"What were you planning to do after you caught her?" continued Reever, his voice low, deadly.

Billy shrugged.

Reever bent, fastened his hand on the boy's shirt and hauled him to his feet and then beyond, dangling the rawboned teenager from his fist and braced arm like a dirty, struggling fish.

"What were you going to do?"

"Not a damn thing! I swear it! I was just havin' some fun with the snotty little—ow! That hurts!"

"Fun." Reever's lip curled in disdain beneath the black slash of his mustache. "Then you must have enjoyed being dumped and dragged behind Blackjack, huh? Wasn't that fun?"

Billy looked away from Reever's pale, narrowed eyes.

"Answer me." Reever's voice was like a lash.

Billy shivered and said, "N-no."

With a single, vicious word Reever opened his hand and let Billy fall to the ground.

"Listen up, boy," said Reever, his tone conversational and his eyes like steel. "You've just hurrahed your last little girl. I kept hoping you'd grow up before I lost my patience, but—" Reever smiled and Billy went as pale as Tory. Reever nodded his head as he saw real fear dawning on Billy. "You're man-sized and snake mean," Reever said matter-of-factly. "I've had a gutful of your dirty mouth and cruel games. If I hear about any more of it, I'll give you the kind of lesson you'll spend a lifetime trying to forget. Hear me, boy?"

Billy nodded sullenly.

"I sure as hell hope you're smarter than you look," said Reever. "That's the only warning you'll get. Stand up."

Billy scrambled awkwardly to his feet. He was almost as tall as Reever but hadn't nearly the hard muscle of the older man. Nor the hard experience.

"I'd have you apologize to the lady," continued Reever, his voice still casual and his eyes utterly savage, "but you wouldn't mean it, and she doesn't want to hear any more of your filth. Now get out of here before I forget how much I liked your daddy and drag you behind old Blackjack until there's nothing left but rope."

With a flick of his wrist, Reever removed the lasso from Billy's shoulders. Reever waited until the teenager was about ten feet away and said, "Pick up her luggage and take it to the Sunup Café. And Billy—"

The big teenager turned around.

"Show me how bright you are," Reever said, coiling the rope again as he spoke. "Make sure that everything of hers is just the way she left it."

Reever watched Billy walk stiffly back to the fence, stopping only long enough to pick up Tory's luggage. While the car speeded away toward town, Reever fastened the lasso to the saddle again and turned to help Tory to her feet. It wasn't necessary. She was already up and walking toward the fence, favoring her right leg slightly.

"What do you think you're doing?" demanded Reever.

Tory wiped her forehead on her dusty arm. "About two miles an hour," she said, smiling crookedly, hoping that he wouldn't hear the faint quaver in her voice. She was over the worst of it now. She simply felt as if she'd spent an afternoon diving in front of hypercritical judges—tired, used up, unsure of herself, determined not to show any of it. She paused and looked over her shoulder. "Thanks. Those kids really had me going."

Reever watched in disbelief as Tory turned away again. He caught up with her in five long strides.

"Where did your car break down?"

"Nowhere. I don't have one."

"Aren't you old enough to drive?"

Tory's hair flashed in the sun as she turned toward Reever quickly, hardly believing what she had heard. A single glance told her that Reever was serious. "I'll be twenty-one this summer," she said tightly.

"Really?" he asked, amusement and relief deepening his voice. He had hated like hell being aroused by someone who appeared as young as Tory. He had always preferred his partners to be as experienced as he was.

Mentally Tory counted to ten and then to twenty. She didn't need Reever's amused glance to remind her that her body wasn't up to the mark for sexy blondes. Most of the time she didn't mind. After all, she didn't want to look like a whacking great milk cow when she dove off the platform. Yet it irritated her unreasonably to know that a man with the raw masculine appeal of Ethan Reever thought of her as a little girl.

"If you didn't drive, how did you get to the ranch?" he asked. His tone was deep, almost lazy, and the steely shade of his eyes warmed as he looked from the delicate curve of Tory's neck to her mouth and remembered how the full bow of her lips had looked when they had parted in silent invitation.

"I came in on the mail truck," she said curtly.

"Where are you meeting Melly for the return trip?"

"Melly?"

"The mail ma'am," said Reever, grinning.

"Oh. Will she be by later on?"

With a feeling of angry disbelief, Reever realized that Tory had not only walked the miles from the ranch house to the county road, but that she had planned to walk the rest of the way to Massacre Creek as well. His hand shot out and he grabbed her arm, stopping her right in her tracks.

"Do you have any idea how far it is to town?" he asked curtly.

"What time is it?"

He answered automatically, frowning. "About one o'clock."

"Then it's about twelve miles to town from here."

The look that passed over Reever's face was indescribable. "Are you crazy?"

"No," she said flatly, meeting his eyes.

What Tory didn't say was that she was hungry, thirsty to the point of spitting cotton and the burning of her raw hands was competing with the throbbing of her knee. She wouldn't say a word about any of it, either. She would quite cheerfully crawl the rest of the way into town rather than whine to the hard-faced cowboy who had taken one look at her, decided she was useless in every possible way and dismissed her with a contempt that still stung.

"Then you're a fool," Reever said harshly. "Or maybe you like swinging your ass down a public highway, just asking for it?"

"*Asking!*" Tory's eyes narrowed as her temper flashed. "You arrogant son of Satan!" she hissed, appalled at herself even as the words escaped her lips. She had taken far worse insults from her coaches, but none of them had been able to set off her temper like Ethan Reever. "I walked down that damned road because there was no other way for me to get into town!"

"If you had told me—" began Reever.

"When?" she interrupted sweetly. "Before or after you turned down my imagined offer of prostitution?"

Reever muttered a few savage words under his breath. Tory didn't bother to listen. She simply turned and marched toward the fence, her back as straight as the line of her mouth. She had heard all she wanted to and then some. It was bad enough to be taken advantage of by a carload of foulmouthed jerks. To be accused of asking for that kind of abuse simply because she was too poor to afford her own car made her furious.

"The next bus won't get to Massacre Creek for three days," said Reever matter-of-factly, catching up to Tory with ease.

She shrugged. Three days, three hours, three weeks. It didn't matter because she didn't have money for a ticket yet. She hoped that the Sunup Café needed a cook or waitress, a dishwasher or someone to clean out the grease trap over the stove. Whatever. She wasn't fussy about honest work.

Reever watched Tory from the corner of his eye. For the first time he saw past the fact that she was female, young and able to arouse his temper and his body with maddening ease. He saw that her thick blond hair was cut simply and that the sun-streaked effect, like her tan, was natural rather than purchased at an expensive salon or resort. She wore no jewelry—no necklace, no bracelet, not even an inexpensive silver ring. The T-shirt she had on was faded and baggy. The slacks were the same and frayed at the cuffs. Her tennis shoes had more holes than canvas and sported no logo from one of the makers of trendy, expensive leisure shoes.

"Wait," Reever said, catching Tory's arm again. His voice was rough, but his hand was gentle on her arm. He had been poor long enough in his youth to recognize the signs. "I'll have one of my men drive you into town."

Tory stared at Reever, her surprise plain. Quite clearly she hadn't expected any help from him.

"For the love of God!" snarled Reever suddenly. "What the hell kind of man do you think would let you walk down a lonely road rather than help you out?"

Before Tory could answer, Reever turned and whistled shrilly between his teeth. Blackjack's ears came up in twin black arcs as the horse trotted obediently to Reever. He mounted in a single flowing motion, kicked his boot out of the left stirrup and looked down at Tory. She was watching him with wide green eyes, looking for all the world like a wind-ruffled, curious cat. He shifted the roping rein to his right hand and held out his left to her.

"Come on."

"Come on what?" asked Tory, looking up at Reever. Way, way up. The horse was as big as a mountain, and Reever wasn't much smaller.

"Get on," he said impatiently.

"How?"

Reever stared at Tory for an instant, not sure that he had heard correctly. He made a sound of disgust, swung his right leg in front of him and over the saddle horn, and slid down to land lightly on his feet in front of her.

"City girl," he muttered. "Useless as teats on a boar hog."

With no more warning than that, Reever picked Tory up and set her down behind the saddle as though she weighed less than a shadow. He put his left foot in the stirrup, swung his right leg up and over the saddle horn and settled securely into the saddle in less time than it took for Tory to realize what was going on. It was obvious that Reever was supremely at home on a horse's back. Despite his size and power he had yet to make a move that wasn't both sure and graceful.

"Hang on."

Tory tried. She grabbed the smooth, raised back of the western saddle with both hands as Blackjack moved off at a pace that seemed terrifyingly fast but was actually no more than a sprightly walk. With each unexpected motion her hands slipped more. The task of hanging on wasn't made any easier by the fact that her blisters had long since broken, leaving her palms raw and oozing a clear fluid mixed with blood. No matter how hard she gripped, her hands kept slipping.

After a few minutes she mastered the rhythm of Blackjack's walk to the point that every movement didn't take her by surprise. She began to breathe more easily. The distance to the ground didn't bother her because she was accustomed to heights, having spent most of her life diving from one kind of platform or another. She would have felt a great deal better, however, if it had been water rather than dirt waiting to catch her if she fell.

Reever sensed Tory's distress and kept the big horse down to a walk. He could have told her to hang on to him but didn't. His hands still burned from their brief contact with her. He had expected her to be soft, and she was. She was also surprisingly firm. If there was any city flab on that young body, he hadn't felt it.

Besides, he was still irritated by her surprise when he had offered to give her a ride into town. If she had decided that he was such a rude bastard that she refused to touch him even to keep her seat, then she could just fall off.

For a long time there was only the muted sound of hoofbeats and the occasional wild cry of a soaring hawk. Blackjack chewed resentfully on the bit that held him to a walk. Reever chewed resentfully on everything that had happened since he had looked up and found a girl-woman standing quietly in front of his desk, setting off his temper and his body with a single look from her faintly tilted green eyes.

When Reever reined Blackjack down the trail to Wolf Creek, the horse shied at nothing more than the shadow of a hawk skimming over the land. Reever moved with the horse like a second skin. Tory didn't. One instant the horse was supporting her bottom and the next instant there was nothing beneath her but air. She grabbed frantically at the saddle, only to feel it sliding out from between her raw palms.

"Reever!"

Even as Tory called out, Reever made a lightning movement, turning and scooping her up in one arm. With a strength that shocked her, he put her back into position behind the saddle using nothing more than a shrug of his shoulders. Blackjack snorted and minced sideways. Tory gasped and grabbed frantically for the saddle again.

"Damn it," snarled Reever, "settle down."

Tory didn't know whether he meant her or the horse. She didn't want to know, either. She bit her lip and tried to guess which way the frisky beast would jump next. Blackjack snorted, then turned and lipped the stirrup as though to ask why they were standing around in the middle of the trail. At a nudge from Reever's heels, the big horse began to trot. Reever didn't need to turn around to know that Tory was losing her balance again.

"Of all the clumsy—" He bit off a curse. "If you can't stand the thought of putting your arms around my waist, hang on to my belt."

Tory looked at the broad spread of Reever's shoulders and the powerful back that tapered down to a lean waist. The thought of touching him made both weakness and a curious heat course through her. Tentatively she lifted her right hand, only to realize that if she held on to him as he suggested, she would get blood all over him. Her frantic attempts to hang on to the saddle had finished the work that carrying her suitcase had begun. Her palms were scraped raw.

"I can't," Tory said in a low voice. "I'll get you—dirty."

"Dirty?" Reever snorted. "Honeybunch, in case you haven't noticed, I'm a rancher, not a damned drugstore cowboy. I'm not going to faint at a little dirt."

Tory's only answer was a choked sound as Blackjack's broad, muscular rump skipped sideways. The horse was just trying to balance Tory's weight more evenly on his back, but she didn't know that. She only knew that she was falling again.

With an exasperated curse Reever dropped the roping rein, reached behind his back with both hands and jerked Tory's arms around him. When he saw the smears of blood across her palms, he knew why she was having so much trouble hanging on to the saddle and why she was afraid of getting him "dirty."

"For the love of God, don't you have any sense at all?" he asked harshly, grabbing Tory's hands and looking at them more closely. Ragged circles of broken blisters showed clearly. The tender flesh was smeared with a mixture of dirt and blood. "Why didn't you say something?"

Tory made a sound that could have been a laugh or a curse. "Then you could yell at me for whining, right?" she said raggedly, furious that everything she did only made Reever more angry with her. "Sorry to spoil your rustic entertainment, but I've been worked over by men who make you look like the tooth fairy. I don't whine or beg or 'swing my ass' for any man, even you. Especially you!"

Reever's whole body tightened as he turned and looked over his shoulder at Tory. Her face was dirt streaked, pale beneath the tan and defiant despite the white lines of fatigue etched around her mouth. Her eyes were a blaze of green fury that was more provocative than any practiced swaying of a woman's hips. Whether she knew it or not, she was crying out to be taken down onto the soft green grass and rolled around until her claws were trimmed and her spitting snarls turned into husky purrs. She would bite and scream at first—and at the end, too. Differently. He knew it, and it made blood gather heavily, hotly, making him bigger with each slamming heartbeat.

"It's bad enough to be so soft, little girl," said Reever in a low voice, "but to be so stupid is dangerous. Don't push me into doing something we'll both regret."

"*Me?* Pushing *you?*" asked Tory, outrage in every syllable. "You—" Her teeth clicked as she snapped her jaw shut. She badly wanted to describe Reever's genetic heritage, most personal habits and certain destination after death, but the only words she could think of had already been used by Billy and his friends. She had no intention of joining their sordid ranks.

"You. Pushing me," Reever agreed flatly.

Lips still parted over words she wouldn't speak and quivering to tell him just what she thought of him, Tory looked straight into Reever's eyes.

It was like diving off a platform as high as the moon. She was falling, twisting, turning, but she wasn't moving at all, everything around her was spinning, and she was motionless, suspended, held absolutely still within his gray glance as heat exploded through her.

The soft, unconscious sound that came from Tory's throat made Reever feel as though he had walked naked into an electric fence. Every muscle in his big body tightened violently. He dragged at breath, aching. The effort it took to control himself shocked him.

"Stop it," grated Reever, unable to look away from Tory's wide green eyes.

"Stop...what?" she asked, her voice husky, her expression dazed.

For a long, seething moment Reever glared at Tory. Gradually he realized that he had been wrong in his assumption that she was one of Payton's pretty toys. Tory wasn't experienced. She didn't understand what was happening between them, what her soft mouth was promising, what her sweet, wild whimper had revealed. She had gotten to him faster and deeper than any woman he'd ever known—and the longer Reever was around her, the more he was afraid that she was a virgin.

"You really don't know, do you?" he whispered, touching the pulse beating rapidly beneath the smooth skin of Tory's throat.

Her only answer was the visible quiver of her lips as she responded to his fingertips caressing her throat. Knowing he shouldn't, unable to stop himself, Reever bent and brushed his mouth over Tory's, breathing in her sweetness, tracing her trembling lips with the tip of his tongue, feeling her pulse go wild beneath his fingertip.

Slowly, very slowly, Reever lifted his mouth from hers, feeling as though he were pulling off his own skin. Her half-closed eyes were a smoldering green, her breath was uneven and her mouth followed his like a compass needle following a lodestone. His breath hissed out in a single savage word as he turned away from her.

"R-Reever?"

"Forget it, honey," he said roughly. "I'm too experienced for a city innocent like you to cut your teeth on."

Tory flinched as though she had been slapped. She wanted to scream at Reever's broad back, to tell him that he was as conceited as he was big, that she wouldn't touch him if he were the last man in the universe. But his single gentle caress had gone through her like lightning, burning away her breath, burning away her thoughts, burning away inhibitions, freeing a surging wildness that frightened her.

Reever held Blackjack to a slow walk, not wanting Tory to have to throw her arms around his hips in order to stay on because what she would find in his lap would have shocked her to her innocent core. He clenched his teeth at the thought of her slender arms sliding around his waist, her fingers testing the power of his thighs and then finding another kind of male power, testing it with her soft hands, measuring the hunger he had for her.

Blackjack tossed his head and minced sideways against the sudden hard pressure of the bit. With a startled sound Tory grabbed Reever. He felt her fingers inside his waistband like a brand. Raging at his own lack of control, he pulled Blackjack up short and dismounted, knowing that he'd never make it back to the ranch at this rate.

"Is that as clean as it looks?" asked Tory.

Reever's head snapped up. "What?"

Tory bit her lip to keep it from trembling, regretting that she had spoken. Everything she did seemed to make Reever furious. Now his eyes were as cold and savage as a winter storm. She swallowed painfully. The dryness of her mouth was a goad, forcing her to speak against her better judgment.

"The water," Tory said huskily. "Is it safe to drink?"

Hard gray eyes glanced toward the creek as though it had just popped up out of the ground. "Yes."

Tory had no stirrup to aid her dismount. Nor did she trust her slippery hands to hang on to the saddle and allow her to ease down to the ground. In the end she did what she had done the first time she had been confronted by a high dive and had become so frightened that she had sat down astride the diving board and refused to move. But she had had to move eventually, just as she had to move now. So she swung her right leg over alongside her left and jumped.

The ground was harder than the water in a swimming pool, and her legs were wobbly from being stretched over Blackjack's powerful back. Favoring her injured knee threw her off balance. She knew that she had a choice between catching herself with her right leg or falling flat on her face. No choice, really. Even as she fell she turned, hoping to take the impact on her shoulder.

Hard hands grabbed Tory and yanked her back onto her feet.

"How anyone as sleek looking as you can be so damned clumsy is beyond me," Reever said in disgust, releasing her instantly. "Or is it just an act to get me to touch you? It won't get you a thing, little girl. I don't believe in on-the-job training."

The only possible answer to that was two words long, and one of those words was at the top of the list that Tory had already forbidden herself to use. Very carefully she walked around Reever and went to the stream. She found a flat, sun-warmed boulder at the edge of the creek, eased herself slowly onto her stomach and lowered her face to the water until she could sip from its silver surface. It was cold, sweet, perfect, like drinking a torrent of winter moonlight. With a husky sound of pleasure, Tory buried her raw hands in the crystal water and lowered her face again, turning it slowly from side to side, bathing away dust and sweat.

Reever watched and felt as though Blackjack had kicked him in the stomach. Tory's sensual pleasure in the water was as wild and pure as the creek itself. As he watched her, he could almost taste the water as she did, could almost feel its bright chill sliding down his throat and caressing his face, washing away dust and sweat, dissolving everything but the sensations of the instant. Without realizing that he had moved at all, he found himself kneeling on the bank just downstream from her, sinking his hands beneath the brilliant silver ripples, wanting simply to be touched by the water that had just flowed over her.

With a savage motion Reever came to his feet, flinging water in all directions, and strode to where Blackjack waited patiently. Tory didn't notice, for her face was still in the sweet water, her eyes closed as she gave her attention completely to the mountain stream that had both slaked her thirst and soothed her burning palms.

"For God's sake," Reever said finally, "what are you trying to do, drown yourself?"

Tory looked over her shoulder at him and laughed, a sound that was as rippling as the water itself. "Cowboy, the day I drown, those sidewinders you once mentioned will be ice-skating in the hottest part of hell."

A corner of Reever's mouth kicked up unwillingly at the image. "You're good in water, is that it?"

"I get by," she said, coming to her feet, wincing slightly as her right knee bumped against the stone.

Unselfconsciously she wiped her face on the hem of her loose T-shirt. Even if she had known that the movement revealed a sleek, tanned strip of her skin from her waist to just below her breasts, she wouldn't have thought anything of it. She was accustomed to being wet and to drying herself on anything handy. She was also accustomed to being all but naked and utterly ignored by the males around her.

Reever frowned, unable to understand Tory's conflicting actions. He touched her and she went off hot enough to burn both of them to the bone, yet she seemed unaware of what she was doing. Although she seemed innocent, she was as unselfconscious as a cat around him. She wasn't immodest; it was just that she seemed unaware of the sensual possibilities of her own body and how easily, how violently, she could arouse men. She was . . . unawakened.

The thought of being the man to awaken her was a sweet agony in his loins.

Tory walked over to Blackjack, who snuffled gently at the damp tendrils curling around her face where her hair had fallen into the water. She laughed softly, delighted by the horse's velvet muzzle and tickling, grass-scented breath.

"What—?" she gasped as she felt herself snatched off her feet without warning.

"Spread your legs," said Reever impatiently.

Speechless, she stared over her shoulder at him.

"God save me from useless city girls," he grated.

His grip shifted. Even as he swung Tory up toward the saddle, his right hand slid down her back, over her buttocks and fastened on the inside of her right thigh, forcing her legs apart. An instant later she was dumped into Blackjack's saddle with about as much ceremony as a hog-tied calf.

"It's called riding stride," Reever bit out. "It's an old custom among us rustics."

Tory's startled, wildly flushed face confirmed Reever's worst fears. She definitely was not used to a man's hands on her sleek body. *Passionate as hell and innocent as heaven.*

A virgin who's too hot to handle. Why me, Lord? he asked bitterly. *Why me!*

"Try not to faint when I get up behind you," he said curtly.

Tory didn't know what Reever meant until he stepped into the stirrup and swung into the saddle as though she weren't already sitting there. With a startled sound she scooted forward, giving him as much room as she could.

The saddle was big—but so was Reever. The saddle was also higher at the front and back than in the middle, a design that helped to keep the rider in place. It also ensured that the only way Tory could rest her weight was smack up against Reever in an intimacy that made her cheeks burn. It made Reever burn, too. His only consolation was that Tory was probably too innocent to know that not all of the hard flesh pressing against her hips was muscle.

It was a small consolation for a problem that would get bigger with each rocking motion that Blackjack made.

"Do we have to—" began Tory, only to gasp as the horse stepped forward eagerly, sending her sliding down into the hot, hard cradle of Reever's thighs.

He heard her breath come in sharply. He saw the shiver of sensation that raced through her, goose bumps clear on her skin. He knew without seeing that her nipples would be rising and tightening, nuzzling against the soft cloth of her T-shirt, searching for a man's caress to ease their sensual ache.

Tory scooted forward again, only to slide back. Grimly she shifted her weight, trying to find a position that wouldn't surround her with Reever's male heat.

"Goddammit," growled Reever, putting his right arm around her hard, pinning her in place. "Stop wiggling!"

"Put me in back again!" Tory said desperately.

"You wouldn't last three seconds."

"But I rode all the way here without—"

Tory's protest ended in a yelp as Blackjack leaped into Wolf Creek with the abandon of a child, dividing the hock-deep water in glorious sheets that sprayed head high on either side of him. Tory clutched wildly at the saddle horn, but it was Reever's steel grip that kept her in the saddle.

Reever tried to be a gentleman and ignore the feel of Tory as his fingers spread wide to hold her in place. But before Blackjack had finished plunging through the creek and up the bank on the far side, Reever knew that Tory's loose T-shirt concealed lush, firm breasts. He also had searing confirmation of his earlier guess—her nipples were as hard as he was and every bit as eager to be touched. The tip of her breast had tightened violently as his fingers accidentally brushed over it when he had to shift his grip at Blackjack's first leap.

Desperately Tory hoped that Reever hadn't heard her gasp when his hand had held her so intimately for just an instant, but there was little hope that he wouldn't notice the flush of embarrassment climbing her neck and flooding her face. She stiffened and leaned away from him, an instinctive reaction that was utterly wrong for the time and the place. She heard him swear violently and wrap his other arm around her to keep her upright in the saddle.

With a combination of fascination and embarrassment, Tory saw Reever's muscular forearm slide beneath her breasts, taking their soft weight, pushing her tight nipples against her water-splashed shirt. Each of Blackjack's rhythmic movements made her breasts sway against Reever's supporting arm. She twisted helplessly, trying to retreat from the intimate contact, but only ended up rubbing against his body even more.

"For God's sake, relax," said Reever harshly. "You've got nothing up top that I haven't felt more of and better."

For an instant Tory couldn't believe what she had heard. Then she believed it. A bitter tide of humiliation washed all the color from her face. She finished the ride to the ranch in absolute silence, counting all the ways it was possible to drown an over-sized, under-mannered cowboy.

Three

———

Reever and Tory rode into the ranch house yard with identical, tight-lipped expressions on their faces. Reever had the edge, though. His black hat, black hair and the harshly masculine lines of his face gave him a distinctly satanic look that Tory's wide-eyed, delicately triangular face couldn't hope to equal. Her eyes, however, matched the devil's in the emotion that made them burn like green flames. By the time the ranch came into sight, Tory had counted sixty-three improbable ways for her to drown a rude cowboy, but she hadn't yet decided how to manage even one of them without touching Reever.

That she refused to do. After she got off Blackjack, she never intended to touch Ethan Reever again.

Tory's stomach growled miserably, audibly, beneath Reever's muscular arm. He cursed under his breath as he realized that she probably hadn't had time for breakfast and certainly hadn't eaten lunch. Then there was always the possibility that, even if she had had the time, she hadn't had the money to buy food. Close up, her clothes were even more frayed than he had first thought.

And there were streaks of blood where barbs had bitten into her tender flesh.

Reever didn't know whether to yell at Tory for being so stupid or to gently lick her as clean as a mother cat would a kitten. One thing he did know—he didn't feel the least bit parental toward Victoria Wells. It had driven him crazy to feel her firm little rump rocking between his thighs. He didn't even feel guilty about her cuts and scrapes anymore. He might not look it, but he was in a lot worse shape than she was. He was steel hard and hot as hell, and his guts were tied in knots from wanting a soft, useless girl with scratches on her back and palms like hamburger. He'd suffered the tortures of the damned on the ride home and had no sympathy to spare for a sweet young thing who wreaked havoc on every male in sight.

Reever cursed softly, steadily, fluently, letting Tory know with each word how very happy he would be to get her off his lap and out of his hair. She ignored him. She had heard a lot of dark muttering during the ride and had promised herself that she would say nothing until she reached the dubious safety of the ranch. Then she would tell Reever just what she thought of him. As the ranch house drew near, she only wished that she had spent more of the ride choosing killing words rather than ways of killing, period.

Blackjack stopped in front of the main corral. Tory's stomach growled vigorously.

"God above," muttered Reever as Tory's stomach rumbled and rumbled and rumbled beneath his arm, "now I suppose you expect me to feed you before I send you to town."

Tory's mouth flattened even more. "Why shouldn't you feed me?" she asked curtly. "You owe me."

"Yeah? How do you figure that?" asked Reever as he dismounted.

The easy power of Reever's movements only made Tory more angry. She knew that her legs weren't going to support her. After she dismounted, she was going to go flat on her face in a sprawl that would only underline Reever's opinion of her. *Clumsy. Useless. City girl.* She gritted her teeth. Why should she care what that muscle-bound, icy-eyed son of Satan thought? She should go down on her knees in the dust and give thanks that she wasn't his type!

"I figure you owe me lunch because you've taken enough bites out of me during the ride for a nine-course meal," Tory said, glaring down at Reever with slitted green eyes.

"Honey," he said coolly, giving her a slow, dangerous, once-over kind of look, "if I'd been nibbling on you, you wouldn't be complaining now—and you sure as hell wouldn't be hungry."

The sensual impact of Reever's eyes and smile made Tory feel as though she were being stroked. She closed her eyes, swallowed hard and muttered, "I thought cowboys were shy, modest and had a vocabulary consisting of 'giddy up' and 'aw, shucks.' But not you, Ethan Reever. You're as proud as Lucifer, and your vocabulary is fully suited to hell."

Reever's mouth turned up in a smile that was very male and frankly threatening. "Keep pushing, green eyes," he said, his voice low, deep. "You'll find out just how hard a man I am."

Blackjack sighed loudly and shifted his weight, hinting that he would like to be in the corral and out from under the saddle.

At the horse's first motion Tory grabbed wildly at the saddle horn, only to wince as her raw palms met leather. Reever cursed softly at the sign of Tory's pain. He jerked off his hat and swept his fingers through his shaggy hair to keep from reaching for her. As she sat up shakily, he yanked his dusty black Stetson back into place, grateful that he wouldn't have to touch her again. The feel of her soft, supple body would tie so many knots in him that he'd be lucky to stand up straight for a week.

"Get off poor Blackjack so he can get some food," said Reever. "He's as tired as I am."

"I don't know what you're complaining about," retorted Tory, delaying the inevitable moment when she would dismount and land in an ungainly heap at Reever's big feet. "You don't ache from your knees to your, uh—"

"Honey, I ache in places you can't even imagine." He watched color climb up Tory's cheeks as his words registered. He laughed softly. "Penny for your thoughts," he offered with a slow smile.

"Go away," Tory said, spacing each word carefully.

"Can't," he said blandly, but beneath his mustache his lips quirked over a hidden smile. "You might need me."

"Like a sidewinder needs ice skates," she said succinctly.

"A sidewinder isn't going to get all rubber-legged from an hour on horseback."

"A sidewinder doesn't have—"

"Legs," interrupted Reever. "Real quick for a city girl, aren't you? Come on, honey. Get it over with. Or can't you even get down alone?"

Tory looked at Reever and brought her running total to sixty-four ways to drown a grinning cowboy. That made her feel better, but it didn't solve the problem of transferring her weight from Blackjack's back to her own feet. She shifted slowly, trying to dismount as Reever had by swinging her right leg over Blackjack's broad rump. As her leg came halfway over, she fished around with her left foot, trying to find the stirrup. It was a long reach because the stirrup length was set for Reever's six-feet-three-inch height.

Belatedly Tory realized that she should have secured her left foot in the stirrup before she started to dismount. It was too late now, though. Her right leg was bumping over Blackjack's rump, her left foot was treading air and saddle leather was racing through her slippery hands. Suddenly her left foot found the stirrup, only to slide right on through the opening as her hands slipped completely off the saddle. The world spun crazily as her left foot went all the way through the open stirrup. She landed flat on her back with enough force to knock out her breath.

Blackjack, who was used to a higher order of skill in his riders, was so surprised that he shied away. Tory was yanked with him because her foot was wedged through the stirrup. Even as the horse moved, Reever leaped for the bridle and hauled Blackjack up short.

"Easy, boy, easy," murmured Reever, calming the animal, for Tory lay half beneath those dancing steel-shod feet.

The thought of what a blow from those hooves would do to Tory's soft body made Reever's blood chill. Despite that his voice was as gentle and firm as his hands while he held the trembling Blackjack still. Tory lay dazed on her back and wondered if that was really Reever's voice, gentle and sweet, deep and soothing, a voice that verified her instinctive belief that there was much more to Reever than his harsh surface. She tried to sit up, to get closer to that reassuring voice.

"Don't move," snarled Reever. "If you spook Blackjack any more with your clumsiness, he'll forget his manners and step all over you."

That voice belonged to Reever, too. Tory had no doubt about it. She had felt its icy lash before. She closed her eyes because suddenly the sunlight was so bright it felt like hot sand beneath her eyelids. She blinked fiercely, wondering why a stupid little fall made her want to cry. It had never been like that in the pool when she was learning a new dive and landed wrong, knocking out her breath and raising livid welts on her skin. She hadn't cried then. Not once.

Maybe it was just that she was so hungry. Maybe that was why she felt as though everything familiar was falling away from her, a row of dominoes kicked over by the doctor's calm description of what had happened to her knee, what might happen again, the future she had worked so hard for toppling in front of her.

Tory didn't bother to look up when she felt Reever's hands easing her foot from the stirrup. She didn't even open her eyes when he swung her up into his arms and began carrying her to the house.

"Are you all right?" he asked roughly.

She nodded and turned her face away from him, hoping he wouldn't see the tears that she felt scalding her eyelids. She wasn't like this. She hadn't cried since she was seven and her father had looked at the first swimming ribbon she had ever won and asked her if third place was the best she could do.

"You sure, honey?"

It was the voice Reever had used to calm Blackjack, warm and gentle and reassuring. It was Tory's undoing. She was accustomed to whip-cracking lectures when she fouled up, not compassion. A shudder went through her.

"Poor little green-eyed cat," Reever murmured, shifting Tory in his arms until her face was tucked against his neck. "This just hasn't been your day, has it?"

Her only answer was the trembling of her body and the hot, silent slide of her tears down his neck.

Reever carried Tory into the ranch house and set her gently in a big oak kitchen chair. "Got your breath back now?" he asked.

"Y-yes."

"Can you sit up without help?"

Tory nodded and leaned back, her eyes still closed. The tears had gone, but she was too embarrassed to look at Reever. He already thought her a clumsy little girl, and she had just proved that he was right in the most humiliating way possible. One corner of her mouth turned down in a bitter smile. It really hadn't been her day.

Yet it had been magic to be held like that, to be cherished by him, if only for a moment.

While Reever ran hot water into a pan, he watched Tory out of the corner of his eye. Beneath her tan she was as pale as a morning glory in moonlight. Her pallor didn't disturb him as much as the sudden quenching of the life in Tory's body that told him she was just about at the end of her rope. Watching her, he knew that he couldn't drive her in to town, dump her at the Sunup Café and drive off. Hell, he didn't even know if she had enough money for the crummy motel at the edge of town. How would she live for the next three days until the bus came in?

Frowning, Reever wrung out a clean cloth in the water, added a mild disinfectant to the pan and carried it over to the table.

"Here," he said, lifting Tory's hands gently. "Soak them in this."

The water was hot without being painful, and the familiar smell of denatured iodine rose from it. It was a favorite disinfectant around the pool because it didn't stain, sting or leave grease floating on top of the water. Tory sighed and sat back again, only to make a startled sound when she felt a warm, moist cloth moving over her face.

"Easy now," Reever said, holding her still. "The war's over, little girl. You're in no shape for any more fighting."

Tory felt both Reever's strength and his gentleness as he cleaned her dusty, tear-streaked face. After the first surprise passed, she made a tiny, inarticulate sound of pleasure and relaxed, giving herself to the unfamiliar luxury of being cared for. Without thinking, she rubbed her face slowly against the cloth and his hand, moving as she had while she bent over the stream.

The hunger that hadn't left Reever since he had first seen Tory sat up and howled. He watched her through narrowed eyes, reassuring himself that she wasn't playing a teasing game with him. She wasn't. Nothing showed on her face but simple, sensual pleasure. She didn't look nearly twenty-one right now. She looked like fifteen, and she made him feel like a lecherous sixty. The longer he looked, the more he became convinced that she had lied about her age.

"I think you better call them," Reever said finally, tossing the wet cloth into the sink and leaning back against the table with his arms crossed, watching her.

"Who?"

"Your parents."

Tory's eyes flew open. "What do you suggest I call them?" she asked flatly.

"Hell, honey, nobody gets along with their parents," Reever said, shrugging. "It's not the end of the world. Call them and tell them you're sorry. They'll be glad to send you bus money to get home."

"How did you know I—"

The words stopped abruptly as Tory realized that Reever had decided she was some kind of teenage runaway. She didn't know whether to laugh or try to drown him in the pan

of water. After a few electric seconds she decided to do neither. She reached with a dripping hand into the frayed
pocket of her slacks and drew out a cloth wallet that was
even more worn than her tennis shoes. The wallet landed on
the table with a soft plop and fell open, revealing a California driving license.

"Read it and weep, cowboy. I may have all the sex appeal of an ironing board, but I'll be twenty-one on my next
birthday. I've been on my own since I was sixteen. I haven't
asked my parents or anyone else for a dime since then."

Reever's eyes narrowed as he measured the change in
Tory. She looked twenty-one now, and then some. He didn't
need to ask if the years had been easy. The threadbare,
empty wallet told its own story. Yet he knew if he offered to
buy her a bus ticket home she would refuse with the same
determined independence that had sent her on a nineteen-
mile walk to town without a whimper.

"An ironing board," he repeated neutrally, raising his
dark eyebrows as he remembered the soft, firm weight of her
breasts nuzzling his forearm. "Honey, they must make some
damned unusual ironing boards where you come from."

Tory looked at Reever's sexy, off-center smile and wondered if he were remembering the long ride to the ranch or
the plunge through Wolf Creek when her nipples had tightened suddenly beneath his hand. He had touched her only
for an instant, but even the memory of it sent heat coursing
through the pit of her stomach.

Tory's breath came in with a soft sound as she saw the
focus of Reever's gray eyes shift from her face to her breasts.
It was happening again, now, right now. She could feel it,
the sudden soft burst of sensation in her nipples as they rose
into hard peaks, stretching and teasing nerves that went
straight to the wild, secret core of her.

"We'd better get them wrapped up," Reever said curtly, turning away before Tory could see his body's reaction to her taut breasts.

Tory stared after him, wondering if he had meant what she thought he meant. As she watched him walk out of the room, she wouldn't have been surprised if he had come back and thrown a bra in her lap. She wasn't wearing one because she didn't own any. For one thing she didn't sag. For another, she was usually in a swimming suit. The overriding factor, however, in her decision to go without that particular piece of clothing had been money. She could appear in public without a bra. She couldn't say the same for a T-shirt or jeans.

When Tory turned and put her hands back into the soothing water, she looked down at her breasts. Instantly she realized Reever must have seen her nipples clearly outlined against the soft T-shirt. She groaned and wondered if she had lost her mind since she had walked out of that doctor's office three days ago. She had been numb since then, an automaton going through the motions of eating and sleeping, and all during the long bus ride here, she had hung on to Payton's letter like a lifeline.

Then the letter, too, had toppled at a touch, one more in a long row of falling dominoes.

A sigh compounded of tiredness, hunger and determination shuddered through Tory. She would find a way to take the months off from diving that the doctor had recommended. She didn't need much in the way of money. There was nothing wrong with her knee that would prevent her from working. If the knee hurt too much, the doctor had told her to take that miracle drug called aspirin.

Strong, gentle fingers lifted one of Tory's hands from the water. Her eyes opened wide, startled. For a big man wearing cowboy boots Reever moved very softly. Eyes that were as clear as rain studied her. She studied him in return, fascinated by the uncompromisingly masculine lines of his face, the high, blunt cheekbones, rugged nose and heavy, wickedly arched eyebrows. Beneath the slightly shaggy mustache his lips were distinctly curved, a sensual contrast with the strong white teeth that showed in his rare smiles.

"See anything you like?" asked Reever dryly, not even looking up from his work on her hand.

Tory realized that she had been staring openly at Reever. She didn't even have the energy to blush or to think of a snappy retort. "You're very handsome," she said simply.

Reever's head jerked up, surprise clear in his eyes. He looked at Tory's expression and realized that she meant exactly what she had said. "That's a first," he muttered and returned to dabbing carefully at her hand.

"Surely women have told you that you're good-looking before," said Tory, feeling uncomfortable.

"Yeah, but never out of bed."

Reever glanced up in time to see the shock on Tory's face. He laughed softly. "You sure you didn't forge that driver's license, honey?"

"You're a—"

"Devil," he finished smoothly. "Yeah, you've pointed that out about once a minute since I hoisted you up on Blackjack."

"I didn't say a word the whole ride."

"You didn't have to. I could feel the anger vibrating through you. Such a passionate little cat. I'm surprised some man hasn't trimmed your claws and tasted all that wild honey by now." Abruptly Reever stopped talking. The direction of his thoughts was having a pronounced effect on the fit of his jeans, not to mention the color of Tory's face. "Don't look so hopeful. I'm not volunteering for the job."

"Listen, you big—" began Tory in a hot voice.

Reever covered her lips with his long, hard fingers, cutting off her tirade. "No, you listen. I'm a man, honey, and I'm used to having women. Women, not girls. If you keep tempting and teasing me, I'm going to grab you and teach you things that will make you blush all the way down to your toenails."

Tory's breath came in and wedged hard in her throat. She wanted to rage against Reever, against what he was saying, to deny every word. But there was truth in what he said, even though she hadn't realized it until that moment. She had taken one look at him and had wanted to get beneath that hard surface to...what? What did she want from him? Why did he have an uncanny ability to set off her temper? Why did just the simple act of being touched by him as he dried her hands and smoothed ointment into her blistered palms make her feel both safe and threatened?

And why was she so certain that in some deep, unknowable way she had been born for the moment when she had opened the Sundance's gate and walked into Ethan Reever's life?

When Tory spoke, her voice was husky, almost ragged. "Normally I'm one of the most even-tempered people you'll ever meet. Ask any of my coaches. But lately..." She shrugged and smiled weakly. "Well, last week was one of the worst I've ever had and having you treat me like a cross between a pushy tart and a juvenile delinquent was adding insult to injury."

"And you were depending on this job, weren't you?" Reever asked gently. "Let me buy you that bus ticket home, honey."

Tory shook her head in a curt negative. "Thanks, but I earn my own way. Always."

"It will be a loan. You can repay it when—"

"No," she interrupted flatly. "It's my problem, not yours. Despite what you believe, I'm a big girl. I've survived much worse disappointments than not being hired by the Sundance Ranch."

There was a taut silence while Reever tried to think of a way to get Tory to accept money. Even as he did, he knew that it was futile. Beneath that smooth, delicate surface she was both proud and determined to make it on her own. He admired those qualities too much to want to fight her over them.

"What happened last week?" asked Reever finally, knowing that he shouldn't. Whatever had driven Tory from Payton's civilized, moneyed circles to the untamed north of Arizona was none of Reever's business, and he knew it. Yet when he had seen the bleakness that had claimed Tory in the instant before she hid it beneath a determined smile, he had wanted to take her into his arms and promise to make everything better. "A man?"

"As in lover?"

"Yes."

"No fair, cowboy," Tory said wearily. "If you want me to stop digging at you, you'll have to stop digging at me. As you've taken pains to point out at every opportunity, I'm not the stuff passionate male fantasies are made of."

"Fishing for compliments?"

"No more than you're fishing for a pan of dirty water in your face," she retorted, anger giving color to her cheeks again. "I know what I am and what I'm not. I'm not sexy."

Reever looked at Tory for a long, long moment and decided that she was telling the truth as she saw it. She didn't believe that she was sexy, period. She was innocent to the last husky breath. And as long as she was that innocent, she could drive him or any other man right over the edge and never know it.

Deliberately Reever lifted his hand and brushed the back of his fingers over Tory's breast. She made a startled sound deep in her throat as her nipple rose tautly. She stopped breathing entirely as his big hand smoothed out the folds of her T-shirt until her hard nipple stood out clearly against the thin cloth. She shivered and made another soft sound.

"That," he said, watching, listening, his expression dark, intense, "is what male fantasies are made of. You respond to a look, a touch, and you make me wonder what would happen if I really looked at you, really touched you."

"Reever, I—" Tory's voice broke as Reever touched her again, softly, so softly, and turned her nerves to lightning.

"Yes," he said. "I know. You want to find out, too. But you're a virgin."

Her eyes widened to reveal a green so pure it made him ache.

"How did you know?" she whispered.

Reever closed his eyes and said something terrible beneath his breath. "I was hoping I was wrong."

He turned away from Tory, traded the tube of ointment for the roll of gauze he had left on the table and began winding the delicate white cloth around one of her palms.

"I'm going to wrap your hands for now," he said, his voice flat. "Tonight, though, be sure to take off the bandages. You'll heal faster in the air."

"Reever," said Tory softly.

"No, honey," he said, not even looking up. "You're too damned young. You'd have to tell yourself that you loved me, and then you'd want me to talk about love, too. That wouldn't happen." He glanced up, pinning her with his hard gray gaze. "I don't lie to women, in or out of bed. I know what kind of woman I'll need before I start talking about love, and I know you're not it."

Tory couldn't believe the sharpness of the pain that went through her at Reever's matter-of-fact words. With a feeling close to fear, she realized how much she cared about him and how many dreams had come into focus at his gentle touch. She could have loved him. She knew it, and it was like dying to know that he couldn't love her in return. She tried to hide her agonized response beneath the flippancy that had allowed her to survive so much in the past.

"Because I'm not small, stacked and sexy?" Tory asked, repeating what he had told her when he had thrown her out of his office.

"Those are qualifications for a roll in the hay, not a gold ring," said Reever matter-of-factly, tying off one ribbon of gauze and going to work on Tory's other hand. "For a wife I want a grown woman who will love me and who will want to have my children, even if I can't promise her city frills and fancies. I want a woman who won't fade the first time the going gets rough. I want a woman who will work beside me on the ranch because she loves the land as much as I do." He shrugged. "I want a woman, not a girl."

Tory closed her eyes and knew that Reever's words shouldn't hurt so much. There was no reason for her to feel as though she were being sliced apart by a razor made of ice. He wasn't deliberately being cruel.

And that was why it hurt so much. He wasn't trying to bait her. He was simply, calmly, telling her the truth. She could turn him on, but that was all she would ever be to him—a roll in the hay, not a woman to love.

For the second time Reever saw the life drain out of Tory and knew that he had caused it. He heard the echoes of his own words in his mind and winced. He had told the truth, but he hadn't thought how it might sound to her, a belittling of her possibilities as a woman.

"Little green-eyed cat," he murmured, touching Tory's cheek with his finger. "I didn't mean that the way you took it. I'm too old for you, that's all. There's nothing wrong with you. You'll find a nice boy who will teach you what it's all about."

"I know all I want to know about boys grabbing and pawing," Tory said in a thin, tired voice.

"That's not what it's all about," said Reever, smiling slightly to himself.

"Yes, I know," she whispered, closing her eyes so that she wouldn't have to see Reever's gentle, very male smile. "But you're the one who taught me that, Reever. Just now, here, in this kitchen." She opened her eyes. "And you're not a boy."

"I'm not going to—" he began tightly.

"I'm not asking you to," Tory shot back. "And I'm not going to ask you. But if you pat me on the head again, I swear I'll bite you."

"I bite back, honey. And you know it, don't you? You like the idea." Abruptly Reever made a disgusted sound. "Hell, here we go again, teasing and baiting and throwing kerosene on the fire. I should know better, even if you don't. Did you ever ask yourself why I keep harping on how damned young you are?"

Eyes wide, the edge of her teeth buried firmly in her lower lip to hold back a hot rush of words, Tory shook her head. Silently Reever pushed back his chair and stood up, no longer trying to conceal what she did to him. Her eyes widened even more as she saw the blunt length of his arousal beneath his jeans. She might be inexperienced, but she was neither blind nor stupid. She knew exactly what that hard bulge of flesh meant.

"My conscience keeps telling me that I shouldn't take you," Reever said flatly. "I don't want to hear a young girl who doesn't know better whispering undying love in my ear. But I want you, honey. I want you like hell on fire. Now do you know what I mean when I tell you not to push me?''

Mutely Tory nodded, trying not to stare at the potent evidence of Reever's masculinity. It was impossible. The thought that she could affect him to that extent made her melt and run like hot, sweet honey.

Reever had expected Tory to be frightened or repelled by his body's frank hunger. He had not expected her to make a swift, soft sound that was halfway between a whimper and a moan, and to look at him as though he were a hidden spring and she was shaking with thirst.

"Sweet God," he said hoarsely. "How the hell did you stay a virgin this long?"

Tory closed her eyes. "It was easy. I hadn't met you." She laughed almost helplessly, and then the laughter faded. She opened her eyes and looked straight into Reever's. "I have too much self-respect to chase a man who wants nothing from me but a roll in the hay. So relax, cowboy. I wouldn't rip your clothes off you, even—" she eyed her trussed palms wryly "—even if my soft little city hands were up to it."

"You're just naturally sassy, aren't you?" Reever asked, smiling against his will.

She laughed slightly, then with genuine humor. "Yeah, I guess so. It's how I stayed sane when the coaches yelled at me. I'd smile and tell them how wonderful they were. Some of them believed me."

Reever laughed out loud, shaking his head. "Coaches, huh? What are you, some kind of tennis baby?"

"Nope. Some kind of water baby. That's how I met your cousin. He's one of the swim club's biggest supporters. He finds jobs for—" Tory bit off the rush of words as she heard Reever's name being called from the yard between the house and the barn.

"In here, Jed," called Tory.

The back door to the kitchen opened, and a man's disgusted voice said, "That lazy son of a bitch Cookie is off on another goddamned toot. If you ask me, when we find him, we ought to string him up by his useless, pea-sized—" There was an instant of shocked silence as Jed spotted Tory. "Er, sorry, miss. I didn't know anyone but the boss was in here."

"No problem," Tory said, smiling at the lean, blond cowhand who looked barely as old as she was. "Where I come from, cussing is one of the favorite outdoor sports."

Jed slanted her a sideways smile. "Yeah? Where you from, pretty lady?"

"Sin City," she said in a husky, theatrical voice, winking at Jed, falling quickly into the kind of kidding that had been a way of life at the swim club.

With narrowed eyes Reever watched the instant, easy camaraderie between Tory and the young cowhand as they introduced themselves. Reever knew that he should be relieved to have those wide green eyes looking anywhere else but at him. He also knew that he wanted to pick up the handsome young Jed by the scruff of his neck and heave him out the back door.

"You bring the cards?" asked Reever curtly.

The buried anger in Reever's voice gave it a crackle that made Jed's head snap around instantly. "No, sir."

"Get a pack while I unsaddle Blackjack and round up the rest of the boys. We'll draw to see who replaces Cookie and who drives him into town."

"Town?"

"Town," Reever said flatly. "This is Cookie's last toot on my ranch. We'll cook for ourselves until I find someone else."

"The boys won't be happy."

Reever grunted.

Tory saw both the distaste and the acceptance in Jed's face. Apparently none of the cowboys liked to cook. Her conclusion was underlined by the banging of the screen door behind Reever on his way out and by the outraged howls of various men as Reever gave them the news.

She hesitated, then turned away from the back door and began rummaging in the kitchen. It was obvious that if she were going to eat anytime soon, she'd have to fix something herself. Humming quietly, she began piling ingredients on the counter by the stove. She looked up from time to time as heated outbursts from the men outside told her that the draw had either been inconclusive or was being hotly contested.

By the time Reever stalked back into the kitchen with the men at his heels, savory aromas were arising from the meat and onions browning in a huge pan on the stove. Tory was working at the counter grating cheese, pausing only long enough to stir the meat from time to time. In a second frying pan, thumbnail-sized chunks of bread were cooking in garlic butter. As Reever walked up behind her, she stretched over the big old stove and shook the pan, making the cubes of bread dance.

"What the hell do you think you're doing?" demanded Reever.

The huge cast-iron pan clattered to the burner, sending chunks of bread flying in all directions.

"Of all the clumsy—" began Reever angrily.

"You're supposed to be a cowboy, not a darned Indian," snapped Tory, cutting off Reever's words. "Why are you always sneaking up on me?"

There were snickers from the six men behind Reever, but nobody said a word. Tory noticed the men for the first time.

"Oh," she said. "Hi." She licked the side of her index finger absently, where garlic butter had run down. "Who lost the draw?"

"Reever," said Jed, unable to hide his smile.

"Oh."

Reever barely heard. His eyes were riveted on Tory's pink tongue licking so delicately over equally delicate skin. He couldn't help but wonder how it would feel to have that hot, sweet tongue caressing him.

Little green-eyed cat. God, she's tying me in knots.

Tory glanced at Reever and saw darkness and anger. "I figured you'd be all day arguing the draw," she said quickly. "I was hungry. So I started cooking."

Reever picked up one of the errant bread cubes, popped it into his mouth and chewed. One black eyebrow lifted in surprise at the unexpected crunch and flavor. He took the spoon and stirred the meat before running his fingertip over the spoon's shallow metal bowl.

"Not bad," he said grudgingly.

"You're too kind," said Tory, her voice as sweet and empty as spun sugar.

As one the cowhands began to fade from the kitchen, sensing with great certainty that the poor fool of a girl was going to set the match to their boss's famous temper.

"Probably," agreed Reever sardonically. He ate several big bites of the meat, apparently impervious to the steamy heat. With a sigh he tossed the spoon back into the skillet. "If I don't die by dinner, you've got a job until you earn enough for a bus ticket home."

"How did you know I was broke?" asked Tory in the instant before she realized that she had been suckered again. As with her virginity Reever had guessed, but he hadn't known until she confirmed it.

"How much money do you have?" he demanded, grabbing her chin when she would have turned away.

"A few dollars."

"A few dollars," he repeated, taking in and letting out a long breath. Then in a deadly voice he asked, "Just how the hell did you expect to get home after you left the Sundance—walk and eat sagebrush?"

"There's always the oldest profession, isn't there?" Tory said flippantly.

Reever's lips flattened. "Honey, you're so clumsy you'd have to give your tricks combat pay."

For the second time that day Tory felt tears clawing at her eyes. She knew that her lips were trembling and hated Reever for seeing it, for shredding her pride until she couldn't conceal her hurt. She hated herself for being so endlessly vulnerable to him. She jerked free of his grasp and turned away before he could see her tears.

Reever swore bitterly. "I told you, little girl. Don't push me."

Numbly Tory nodded, grating cheese blindly.

"If you want the job, I'll have Dutch pick up your stuff when he dumps Cookie," Reever said, his voice harsh.

Tory knew that Reever wanted her to refuse. She wanted to refuse, too. But she had no choice. She hadn't seen a Help Wanted sign anywhere in Massacre Creek. Today, like so many times in the past, she couldn't afford the luxury of pride. She had to take what was offered and smile and make the best of it. Normally it didn't bother her. It did now.

She took a deep breath before she spoke, afraid that her voice would shake. She didn't want that. She would die before she showed Ethan Reever any weakness again.

"Yes," she said finally, quietly. "I want the job."

Reever watched the slender, proud line of Tory's back for a long time, cursing silently. He had seen the too-brilliant

green of her eyes and the betraying quiver of her hands as
she worked. He stalked out of the kitchen, yanking his hat
into place and letting the screen door bang loudly behind
him, cursing himself thoroughly—and hoping to God that
he could keep his hands off Tory until she earned a bus
ticket back to the city, where she belonged.

Four

―――――

"**I**'ll do it, Jed," said Tory, reaching for the egg basket that the young cowboy was holding.

"You sure?" he asked. "That one-eyed hen is as mean as a snake. She's pecked Reever more than once."

"And survived to lay another egg?" Tory asked dryly. "You should cast that feathered phenomenon in bronze."

Jed laughed and looked at Tory with lively blue eyes. During the three weeks that she had been on the ranch, the men had come to enjoy her quick tongue as much as her cooking. All except Reever, of course. Jed didn't know what had happened in the kitchen that day when the hands had slunk out, leaving Tory to face the boss in the full flare of his devil temper. But Jed knew that since that day Tory hadn't done anything in Reever's presence except be cheerful, prompt with meals and a very hard worker.

"Sure I can't talk you into a movie tonight?" asked Jed wistfully. "That old kitchen will come apart if you clean it one more time."

"I'm sure. But thanks, Jed," she said, winking at him. "It's nice of you to ask a senior citizen."

Jed winced and then laughed, shaking his head. "Hell, Tory, I'm only two years younger than you." He looked at her suddenly. "You got a guy back home?"

"No." Tory hesitated and then said simply, "I don't want one here, either. I'll go to a movie with a bunch of the hands, but not with just one. I'm a friend, not a date."

Jed sighed. "Okay," he said finally, "if that's the way you want it."

"Thanks for understanding," she said, smiling in return.

"You watch out for that old hen," Jed repeated, walking off toward the corral. "She's been a real terror lately."

Tory walked out to the henhouse, swinging the basket from her arm, grateful that Jed had decided to look for romance elsewhere. With the Sundance hands, Tory had quickly established the easy, humorous camaraderie that had been the hallmark of her relationship with the various boys and men who had shared the swim club's huge pools. The inevitable sexual innuendos of the cowhands were either ignored or topped with a deadpan innocence that had caused more than one man to choke into his napkin with disbelief and laughter. Invitations for dates were turned down quickly, firmly and with a pleasant smile. Tory didn't want to be a challenge to the men. She wanted to be a sister.

Reever was the only exception to that rule. Tory wanted to be more to him, but she knew that it wasn't going to happen. She tried to accept the bittersweetness of finding for the first time in her life a man she could have loved and then losing him before she ever had a chance, simply because she had been born in the wrong place and years too late to attract him. It wasn't fair to lose that way, through circumstances that she had never controlled, but that kind of loss didn't surprise her. Life simply wasn't fair. She had learned that the hard way in the past, when judges were capricious or outright biased in choosing the best divers. Win some. Lose some. Some never had a chance. Maybe next time luck would break her way.

At least, that's how she had always consoled herself in the past.

All around Tory sunshine poured down from a sky so blue that it almost hurt to look at it. There were a few fluffy clouds skidding about, chased by a wind that never touched the ground. The smell of new growth and damp earth swirled invisibly around Tory. She took a deep breath, savoring the sweetness of the air, feeling herself expand into the limitless land. She loved the early mornings when the world was fresh and the Sundance's sweeping vistas brought a feeling of peace to her that she had never experienced before she had come to the ranch. Nerve endings and muscles that she hadn't known were tight had slowly relaxed through the weeks, leaving her with a feeling of contentment that was like coming home.

Even Ethan Reever's satanic temper and razor tongue hadn't been able to spoil that.

After a lifetime of buying perfectly matched eggs in cold, sterile plastic cartons, Tory found the gathering of various sizes of eggs still warm from the nest to be satisfying in a way that she couldn't describe. She couldn't have enjoyed collecting the eggs more if they had been brightly colored and full of Easter chocolate.

"Morning, you ugly, one-eyed witch," said Tory cheerfully, pouring feed into the small troughs that ran along the exterior of the henhouse.

The hen in question gave Tory an evil look before going to work pecking at the feed through the fence. The other hens followed suit with only a small flurry of clucking and flapping. They were getting used to Tory as she slowly took over the lighter chores, freeing Jed for other work. When she was sure that the hens were busy, Tory climbed up the rickety old stepladder leaning against the coop's outside wall. She opened the small door that would give her hands access to the raised nests and wedged her upper body into the henhouse while she patted through the warm straw in search of eggs. She couldn't see much inside the dark coop, but she didn't need to. Her fingers could find the eggs faster than her eyes.

As Tory pulled out eggs one by one and put them into the basket she had braced between her feet, she thought covetously of the small patch of land just in back of the house. Sometime in the past that patch had been a kitchen garden. She was sure of it. The suggestion of neat furrows was subtle yet distinct, and she had found the remains of a compost pile behind the chicken house. She had never had any time to garden as a child, yet the thought had always tempted her. Growing seeds into whole plants, eating the fruits or vegetables that unfurled so miraculously from such vulnerable beginnings, taking part herself in the advancing of the seasons across the earth—she wanted to do that. She wanted to touch the land and feel it warm and fertile beneath her hands.

Tory was so caught up in dreaming about a garden that she was slow to collect the eggs. The first warning she had that something was wrong was a sharp pain, as though someone had rammed a thick thorn into her finger. With a gasp she jerked her hand away, upsetting her precarious balance as she leaned into the coop. Her feet kicked over the basket of eggs as she tried to right herself without using her hands, which were shielding her face from the one-eyed hen.

Tory succeeded in protecting her eyes but only at the cost of getting her hands severely pecked. She tried to back out but couldn't without uncovering her face. Frantically, blindly, she braced her weight on her elbows and tried to grab the mean hen. The wild battle stirred up the rest of the chickens. Some of them joined in the effort to repel the intruder. Others simply rushed around clucking and screeching as though a coyote had slipped into the coop and was eating them one by one.

Reever heard the noise, came out of the barn where he had been checking on a lame horse and saw Tory struggling half in and half out of the henhouse. With five running strides he was there. His big, leather-gloved hand shot over Tory's shoulder, covering her face as he yanked her out of the one-eyed hen's reach and slammed shut the high, narrow opening.

"You clumsy little city idiot," he said roughly, setting Tory on her feet amidst the broken eggs. "Look at that mess! I should take a whip to Jed for not warning you about that one-eyed hen!"

Tory tried not to flinch from the icy contempt in Reever's eyes. "Jed warned me. I was just slow getting the eggs."

She took a step backward, then another, retreating from Reever's black presence. She had managed to get along with everyone at the ranch but its big, harsh-faced boss. No matter what she did, how well she did it or how careful she was to be cheerful and respectful of Reever at all times, he had ridden her mercilessly about her youth, her softness and her unfamiliarity with the ranch. She didn't want to give him another verbal stick to beat her with. She had to reach the kitchen and get her hands cleaned up before he noticed them.

"It was my fault," Tory said quickly. "You're right. I'm clumsy. I'm sorry. You can take the eggs out of my pay. I'd better get back to the kitchen," she continued as she turned, trying to use her body to shield her painful hands from Reever's glance as she moved. "I don't want the beans to burn."

Tory knew the exact instant when Reever saw her fingers. His body went absolutely still, then his hands shot out and fastened around her wrists. The words he said made her wish that she could fall right through the ground. She tried not to show it. She had decided to treat Reever like the hardest coach she had ever had. No matter how sarcastic, how cutting, how cruel he was, she would be unfailingly agreeable, never argue and never, ever show how badly she was being cut up.

"Where the hell are the leather gloves I told you to get?" finished Reever with a snarl.

Mentally Tory braced herself and said quietly, "I didn't buy them."

"What?"

"I didn't buy them."

"Why not?"

For a long moment Tory said nothing, knowing that her next words would set off Reever's famous temper but good. The job as cook wasn't high-paying work. There was no reason for it to be; room, board, laundry, almost everything was paid for by the ranch. She was given a small—very small—weekly salary. Out of that she had already bought shoes, socks, a new T-shirt and a pair of jeans to replace the clothes that had been ruined the day she had tried to walk to town.

Nor did the expenditures end there. She had had to buy anti-inflammatory medicine and elastic bandages for her knee, soap, lotion, shampoo, toothpaste and intimate feminine items. By the time she had bought the necessities, there was nothing left, not even enough to pay her way in to a movie in town. The leather gloves that Reever had ordered her to buy would cost the equivalent of half a week's pay.

"I'll look for gloves the next time I'm in town," said Tory, knowing that "look" was all she would be able to do. She could barely afford to renew her prescription for her knee. Then there was the second set of weights she had ordered to allow her to continue strengthening her knee. They were coming COD. She had to be able to pay for them. She couldn't do that if she bought the gloves.

"I didn't tell you to buy them next week," retorted Reever. "I told you to buy them two weeks ago when you started stumbling around after the men in the barn and the corral. Remember?"

"Yes, sir."

The formality wasn't sarcastic, it was a reflex left from years of being coached by overbearing males. Reever didn't know that, however. His eyes narrowed as though Tory had slapped him.

"Just plain Reever, city girl. Think you can remember it, or should I have that hen tattoo it on the back of your soft, useless hands?"

"I'm sorry, Reever," said Tory tightly, struggling to keep her voice from breaking.

He stared at Tory's downcast eyes, but she neither moved nor looked up at him. She had been like this since that first day in the kitchen—polite, respectful, trying very hard to please. And the harder she tried, the more angry he became.

Tory realized it but didn't know what she could do. The verbal punishment Reever had given her for her flip remark about taking up the oldest profession still made her pale with humiliation every time she thought about it. So she stayed polite and cheerful and prayed that sooner or later he would get tired of peeling strips off her, or she would be able to save enough for that bus ticket home.

Only it wasn't home she would be going toward, and Tory knew it. It was simply the only place she had left to go.

"Wash your hands," Reever said in disgust. "I'll have one of the men drive you into town so a doctor can look at them."

Tory stared at Reever. "But when Jed got that wicked rope burn, you didn't make him go to town. Why should I go for a few lousy pinpricks?"

Reever's mouth flattened until there was nothing but a tight line beneath his black mustache. He held Tory's hand up to her face as though the fingers were separate condemnations. Blood trickled from the various small wounds the hen had inflicted. "Jed isn't a soft little girl."

"Neither am I," Tory said, fighting to keep her voice even.

"I said go and you'll go."

"I can't," she said. "I'm sorry. I can't afford a doctor."

In silence Reever examined the thoroughly pecked flesh on Tory's hands. "Is that why you didn't buy gloves?" he asked finally.

She hesitated, then nodded.

When Reever's eyes shifted up to Tory's face, she couldn't help flinching. Seeing that didn't make his temper any softer. Or his tongue. "Then maybe you should have spent less money painting the town red with the boys," he said harshly.

Tory stared, her green eyes wide with disbelief. "What?"

"Do you think that I didn't notice all of you piling into Smitty's car on Saturday afternoon and not coming back until early Sunday morning?"

Tory closed her eyes, telling herself that she could not, simply could *not,* let her temper slide out from under her control. "It was Dutch's birthday."

"Yeah, I heard. Was it a Dutch treat all around," continued Reever sardonically, "with you doing the treating and the boys doing the paying?"

All the words Tory couldn't say crowded her throat. She pulled her hands free of Reever's grasp and said, "I'll buy gloves as soon as I can afford them."

"Better buy a face mask, too, city girl. That old hen will peck your eyes out next time," retorted Reever.

He watched Tory's retreat with narrow, steel-colored eyes. When he looked down at his scarred leather gloves and saw her blood on them, he swore savagely. Abruptly he kicked aside the egg basket, climbed the stepladder and opened the henhouse door.

As Tory soaked her hands in a pan of warm, iodine-tinted water, she heard another wild squawking from the henhouse. It ended before she could see what was happening. An hour later Jed came into the kitchen, carrying the egg basket.

"Boss says he wants chicken and dumplings for dinner."

"I'll check the freezer," said Tory, "but I think I fried the last chickens for Sunday lunch."

"No problem," said Jed, reaching into the basket and tossing the plucked, cleaned and rather lean body of a chicken on the counter.

Tory gave him a startled look.

Jed grinned. "Guess the 'feathered phenomenon' pecked the boss once too often. He wrung her neck and cleaned her himself." Jed spotted Tory's hands. "Holy cow, Tory. What—oh, Lord! It wasn't Reever the hen got, was it?"

She smiled crookedly. "Like Reever says, I'm clumsy."

"Clumsy?" said Jed with an incredulous look at her. "You're about as clumsy as the cat when she's prowling for mice in the barn."

"Yeah, sure," Tory said, grimacing.

Her mouth turned down as she remembered all the times she had made a fool of herself in front of Reever—most recently at the henhouse. She had no illusions as to how graceful she had looked with her fanny hanging out of the chicken coop and her legs kicking air. Sighing, she picked up the big hen gingerly. It was one thing to gather eggs that were still warm. It was quite another to confront a barely cooled chicken carcass.

"Pretend you just unwrapped it from the store," offered Jed, grinning at Tory's obvious discomfort.

She smiled weakly and began filling a big pot with water as Jed closed the screen door behind him. While the hen simmered on the stove, Tory found the old ranch cookbook that had become her bible in the last few weeks. Being a short-order cook hadn't given her a very large list of specialties. While her pancakes had been wonderful, her biscuits could have been used to shoe horses, as Reever had pointed out. She had kept trying, working when no one was around, until she had learned how to make a tender, savory biscuit. The men had complimented her extravagantly. Reever had said nothing but "Pass the butter."

It had been that way with everything. If she did it badly, he let her know in no soft terms. If she did it well, he ignored her. Dutch had told her that it was nothing personal—Reever was like that with everybody. But even Dutch had to admit that Reever gave Tory less slack and more spur than anyone else in the outfit.

Tory's solution had been to work longer and harder, just as she had done at the swim club, hoping that sooner or later Reever would let up. In the past even her toughest coach had acknowledged it when she had done a good job.

But not Reever. It seemed that the harder she worked, the more sarcastically critical he became.

Nothing personal.

Tory wished that she could believe it. She wished that she could forget all the times that Reever had cut her to the bone with his caustic appraisals of her as a cook, egg collector, dishwasher—and woman. That most of all. The memory of how her breasts had risen eagerly to his touch humiliated her to her core. Even now he had only to look at her and she felt it starting all over again, the shivering, melting fire.

Honey, you're so clumsy you'd have to give your tricks combat pay.

Nothing personal? Yeah. Sure.

Gloomily Tory began to read the recipe for chicken and dumplings. For once she had all the ingredients on hand, including an old, tough hen.

Throughout the day Tory hovered over the stew pot, tasting, poking, adjusting herbs and salt as the cooking progressed. The chicken itself had a fine flavor that kept improving as the hours passed. When it was time for the dumplings, Tory did everything according to the book, bit into a dumpling and knew she was in for the cutting edge of Reever's sarcastic tongue.

With a sinking heart she threw out the first batch and made more dumplings, measuring the flour so scrupulously that she all but counted each particle. The result looked and tasted like what it was. Boiled dough. Unfortunately the dumplings were the backbone of the meal, for one chicken divided among nine mouths didn't go very far, even when that chicken was formerly the biggest, meanest hen in all of Arizona.

As Tory set the table, she braced herself for the ordeal to come. The chicken was tender and flavorful, quite the best that Tory had ever tasted, although she had to admit that revenge might have been part of the savor—her hands still hurt from the punctures and bruises the hen had inflicted. The vegetables she had cooked were just right, firm rather than mushy, with a scattering of herbs to bring out their natural flavor.

But the dumplings still tasted like boiled dough.

The men piled into the kitchen as Tory was pouring the thick, lethal coffee that they all loved and she could barely swallow.

"Evening, Tory," said Dutch, hanging his battered hat on a knob projecting from one of the old oak chairs that surrounded the scarred wooden dining table. He slid into his chair eagerly. "Been smelling this all day. Driving me crazy, it smells so good."

The others were right on Dutch's heels. Within moments the big kitchen was full of hungry men. One of them was Reever. He gave Tory's hands a long glance as she poured his coffee. His eyes narrowed at the sight of the small, livid wounds dotting her fine-grained skin.

"Jed," said Dutch, "you better check the henhouse after dinner. When I went by on the way in, that one-eyed hen didn't come out to peck at my boots through the wire. She might be sick."

"Nope," Jed said confidently, helping himself to chicken and dumplings. "That crazy old biddy done pecked her last," he drawled.

"Yeah?" asked Dutch, forking a chunk of chicken into his mouth. "Lord, Tory, you're gonna spoil us," he said, closing his eyes and chewing slowly. "Best chicken I ever had." He sighed and turned his attention back to Jed. "What happened?"

"Reever wrung her neck," said Jed succinctly.

Dutch looked at his dinner plate with new interest. "I'll be damned." He looked at Reever. "Hell, boss, I thought you said you'd never touch one feather on that mean old—"

"Are you going to talk or eat?" interrupted Reever.

Tory stared at Reever, wondering if that really could be a dull red climbing up his blunt cheekbones. Quickly she glanced away, concentrating on pouring Dutch's coffee without spilling a drop. She didn't need another of Reever's cutting lectures on her clumsiness.

"I can eat and talk at the same time," Dutch said, grinning. "What changed your mind about that crazy old hen? Did she peck your favorite horse? Did she—" Dutch's baiting words stopped abruptly when he saw Tory's hands hovering over his coffee cup. He muttered something under his breath and shot Reever an approving glance before looking back at Tory. "The boys and I will take turns on the dishes until you're healed. Ma always said there's nothing worse than dirty dishwater for infecting cuts."

"That's all right, Dutch," said Tory quickly. "I'll just put iodine on my hands afterward."

"Hell, girl, don't be silly," Dutch said, his voice gruff. "Who sewed up the rip in my new shirt so good I couldn't even see the mend? Who spent half the night writing letters to the government for Teague and Miller so they wouldn't be shamed by their spelling in front of city folks? Who's been changing the dressing on Smitty's best horse so that the cut heals twice as quick? Who's been—"

"Pass the dumplings," Reever said coolly, cutting across Dutch's words.

Tory heard the anger vibrating in Reever's curt command and wondered what was wrong now. As she handed him the dumplings, she realized that whatever was riding him would soon be supplanted by the uninteresting taste of her dumplings. She watched his strong white teeth bite into a creamy lump of cooked flour and braced herself for the worst.

Reever grunted, heaped more dumplings on his plate and resumed eating.

Tory almost dropped the coffeepot in her astonishment. She watched the other men from the corner of her eye as she finished pouring coffee. They attacked the dumplings with every evidence of pleasure, complimenting her between bites. With a soundless sigh, she took her place at the table and ate a bite of dumpling herself, wondering if it had somehow been miraculously transformed by the trip from the stove to the table. A single bite told her that nothing about the dumpling had changed. She'd eaten tastier library paste.

Thank God that Reever hadn't.

Tory ate slowly, ignoring the dumpling, listening to the men talk about how the range was greening at the higher elevations as spring progressed up the steep slopes of Blue Wolf Mountain, which comprised the northwestern half of the Sundance. All the talk of spring and growing things reminded her of the garden she wanted.

"Jed?" she asked quietly, catching his eye. "Are you going into town soon?"

"Early tomorrow morning. Need something?"

"Seeds."

Although Tory had tried to keep her voice down, she sensed Reever's sudden interest.

"Sure. What kind of flowers you want?"

"Beans, tomatoes, peas, squash, parsley, onions, carrots." Tory paused for breath. "Corn, too. Do you think I can grow corn out back?"

Jed shrugged, smiling. "Beats me. I couldn't grow a toadstool if I tried."

Tory didn't really hear him. She was remembering the last time she had stood in a supermarket in South California, slowly turning a rack of seed packets with her hand, watching the brightly colored pictures flow by with a hunger that she was just now understanding.

"Zinnias," she murmured. "And sweet peas and marigolds and daisies and—" She laughed suddenly. "Oh, all of them, Jed. Every seed you can buy. I want to plant them all, watch those first tiny shoots push up from the ground, see all the different shapes of leaves and flowers." Abruptly Tory remembered that seeds weren't free. Some of the vivid pleasure faded from her expression. "Well, not all at once, of course." She smiled crookedly. "About three dollars' worth to start, okay?"

"You got it," said Jed.

"Where are you going to plant all that?" asked Reever, looking at Tory with an expression that she didn't understand.

"Out back where the kitchen garden was."

"'Was' is right," Reever retorted sardonically. "That ground hasn't been touched since my grandmother Abby Reever died a half century ago. After her the Reever and Sundance wives lived in the city. They sucked the ranch dry buying store beef and fancy clothes, and they wouldn't have dirtied their fingernails in a kitchen garden to save their lives. City girls every one of them."

Contempt resonated in Reever's voice. Every year he managed the ranch for his aunts and his cousins, dividing the hard-won profits with them. Fifty-five percent to the

Sundance family, including Payton, who had earned a fortune investing the money elsewhere. Forty-five percent to Reever, who reinvested every penny in the ranch itself, even though his was not the deciding vote in how the ranch was run. Payton could, and had, forced Reever to build the Sundance Retreat up on Wolf Lake. Reever had given in finally because he knew that Payton would lose interest in the retreat after a few years. Then the beautiful cedar lodge and outbuildings would make a perfect center for the ranch, miles closer to the road than the present ranch house.

One day the Sundance would be Reever's, all of it. Until then Reever's "pay" every year for managing the ranch for his aunts and cousins was another one percent ownership of the ranch that nobody else in his family wanted. They wanted the money that the ranch yielded beneath Reever's sweat and skill, though. His aunts wanted to be carried on Reever's broad back so that they'd never have to work. And it had happened just that way.

"City girls," muttered Reever, forking chicken and dumpling into his mouth. "Useless."

Tory had to bite her lip to keep from pointing out that being from the city didn't ensure that a woman was lazy any more than being from the country ensured that a man was a hard worker.

"Tell me, city girl," Reever continued, pinning Tory with a metallic glance. "How are you going to prepare the ground for all those seeds?"

"I saw a shovel in the barn," she said neutrally.

"You'll have to do a hell of a lot more than *look* at a shovel to get a garden," he retorted. "Or did you just expect to plug the shovel in and watch it dig all by itself?"

Tory swallowed a crack about not being able to find an extension cord that long. "No," she said quietly. "I expected to get it done one foot at a time."

"Left or right foot?" asked Jed innocently.

Tory tried not to smile but didn't succeed. "Whatever works," she said, giving Jed a sideways glance out of eyes as green as gems.

Reever caught the look, and his mouth flattened until there was nothing except a thin, hard line. But whatever he was going to say was lost beneath the genial argument over whether it was better to shovel with the left or the right foot. Tory listened to the men with relief, hoping that Reever had been deflected from another scathing speech about useless city girls. She didn't know how much longer she could hold her tongue, especially when being polite was a one-way street. She couldn't bait Reever or even respond to his baiting, but he was under no such restraints with her. If he wanted a bite out of her, he just took it and dared her to bite back.

And she was terrified that she would. Then she would lose, and lose hard. She could all but taste the scalding humiliation that would come if she crossed Reever.

Quietly Tory pushed back her chair and began to clean the kitchen while the men finished dinner. Normally she enjoyed sitting around the table with them, listening and learning as they talked about horses and cows, grass and creeks, storm and sunshine. She didn't want to stay around tonight. Reever was in a savage mood, his features bleak and unforgiving. Sooner or later she would bear the brunt of his temper unless she got out of his sight.

When Dutch started to object as Tory took his plate, she bent closer and whispered, "Don't get up. Please, Dutch. Reever will skin me alive. My hands are okay. Really."

Dutch muttered something fully suited to Reever in his worst mood, but the wiry little cowhand didn't get up and help Tory with the dishes. Dutch, too, had seen the black signs of Reever's temper. So had the rest of the hands.

Within minutes the kitchen was empty but for Tory and Reever. To her relief he got up and went into his office to work on the books. Tory sighed unconsciously and wondered if Reever's temper would be any better the following morning.

It wasn't. None of the hands escaped the caustic effects of Reever's tongue. Tory waited until he had ridden off before she went out to the barn, found an old shovel and went to work on the garden.

And work it was. The ground was rich but stubborn. The shovel was heavy and better suited to boots than tennis shoes. Dutch came by with a pair of his old work gloves in his hand. They were big on Tory, but they made it much easier to handle the splintery old shovel. Even so, she had done only one short furrow by the time she had to go inside and begin lunch. The ragged line of earth glistened with fertile promise each time she looked out the window.

One time when she looked out, the line of turned earth had suddenly, impossibly widened. She blinked, shook her head and stared. From the back porch came the sound of Jed's and Dutch's voices. Then came Miller's. She raced to the other window and saw the three cowhands making short work of the earth. Two of them used spades that sliced easily through the ground. The third broke up the big clods with the shovel.

"Reever's gonna tan our hides," said Jed casually.

Miller grunted, rubbed a weathered leather glove over his equally weathered jeans and spat a stream of tobacco juice off to one side.

Dutch shrugged. "I figure it this way, son," said the cowhand, leaning on the spade. "Reever told us to shovel out the corral. Now, if we want to shovel them sunbaked turds into this patch of ground instead of off behind the barn, that's our business." There was a pause, then, "Move it, Miller. Here comes Teague with another wheelbarrow of Blackjack's best.''

Tory watched until tears blurred the men into shadows. Slowly she turned back to the chili that was simmering on the stove. She wiped her eyes impatiently as she opened the flour bin. She had been practicing piecrusts for two weeks. Now was as good a time as any to see if she had learned to make a crust that tasted better than it looked.

By lunchtime the smell of apple pie was competing with the spicy fragrance of chili. As she pulled the second pie out to cool, she looked at the crust critically. Not gorgeous, but acceptable. And she knew the pie itself would taste good because she had eaten a spoonful of filling when she cleaned the bowl. Now all she had to do was find out if the hands liked cheese or ice cream with their hot apple pie.

Tory went to the back door. As she reached for the handle, the sound of Reever's voice came clearly through the screen.

''What do you think you're doing?''

''Shifting turds,'' Dutch said succinctly.

Reever's ice-pale glance went from man to man. Without a word he turned Blackjack and went back to the corral. Tory let out a long breath and crept silently back to the kitchen. When the table was set, she went out to the metal triangle that hung from the porch roof. She banged enthusiastically with a steel wand, calling the hands in to lunch.

No one came running. Frowning, she banged some more. Still no one. She walked out into the yard, looked around, but saw no one. Slowly she climbed the steps onto the back porch and walked into the kitchen, wondering where all the men were.

Everyone was in place around the table but Reever. All of the men were trying so hard not to smile that their faces must have ached. Bewildered, Tory looked from one to the other, wondering what was going on. Then she spotted the mound of small, colorful packets heaped to overflowing on her plate. Seeds and more seeds, a cascade of possibilities calling to her. There were so many—far more than three dollars could have bought.

"They're all yours, Tory," said Jed, grinning and sliding three dollar bills under her plate. "And if you try to pay us back, we'll pour cement in your garden."

With an excited sound Tory hurried to the table, feeling like a kid on Christmas morning. She didn't see Reever silently close the porch door behind him. He leaned a hard shoulder against the doorframe, stuck his thumbs through the loops of his jeans and watched while surprise and pleasure transformed Tory's face. She ran her fingers through the piled packages of seeds as though they were gold and jewels, reading off the names while her voice got more and more husky until it shivered into silence over her words of thanks.

"City girl," said Reever curtly, "I think you and the boys have forgotten something."

Tory started, scattering bright packages over the table. She looked over her shoulder almost fearfully. "Oh, Reever, please," she said, her voice husky. "Let me use that little bit of land. I won't let it get in the way of my cooking."

"Hell," Reever said roughly, hating to hear the catch in Tory's voice, "you can have the damned garden, for what good it will do you."

"What do you mean? Isn't the ground good?"

"The ground's fine. You're the problem, city girl," he said, looking straight into Tory's pleading green eyes. "You're not going to be around long enough to see any of those seeds bloom, are you?"

Tory looked at the bright faces of the packets scattered across the table and knew that Reever was right. She had forgotten that the Sundance wasn't her home and that Reever had made no secret of the fact that he wanted her out of there at the earliest possible moment.

"I guess not," she said sadly, blinking back tears. "So I'll just have to enjoy as much of it as I can, won't I?"

There was no answer but that of Reever's hungry, steel-colored eyes watching Tory's fingertip trace the bursting ripeness of the tomato pictured on a package of seeds.

Five

────

Flexing her hands, Tory looked down at the supple yet sturdy work gloves she wore. They had appeared by her breakfast plate two weeks ago. The cowhands had all denied any knowledge of how the gloves had gotten there. When she had put the price of the gloves in cash on the dinner table the following week, the money had stayed there for three days before she gave up and put it back in her wallet.

The golden-brown, rough suede surface of the gloves was already stained by dirt from the garden and scratched here and there by angry hens, baling wire and barbwire. Tory was spending more and more time in the barn and around the corrals. Despite her rather hard initiation into riding, she found herself fascinated by the horses. Dutch and Jed swore that she had a knack for handling the big animals. The hands had taught her how to groom, bridle and saddle horses, as well as how to rake out a stall. She had gradually taken over the care of the horses that turned up lame or cut, as well as the calves that had been injured in one way or another.

If Reever objected to Tory caring for the animals, he had said nothing to her about it. That was what had given her the courage to wheedle riding lessons out of Jed. She was no longer satisfied with just being around horses. She wanted to be able to ride out over the land and feel the wind in her hair. She wanted to know again the pleasure of a horse's easy rocking motions, a pleasure that she had tasted a few times during that long ride to the ranch with Reever. She needed to be outside, moving; she was accustomed to more strenuous exercise than being cook for the Sundance's eight men. She was . . . restless.

Jed rode into the yard, spotted Tory in the garden and smiled. "Soon as you're finished fooling around in the dirt, come to the main corral."

"Are you sure you have time?" asked Tory eagerly, almost afraid to hope. Every time they had planned a riding lesson, Reever had piled more work on Jed.

"I got a head start on my work today," Jed said, yawning. "I've been riding fence since first light."

Suddenly Tory realized why the young cowhand hadn't been at the breakfast table or in for lunch, either. "Oh, Jed, I didn't mean for you to—"

"I'll forgive you if you bring a sandwich with you," interrupted Jed. "And you might bring a carrot for Twinkletoes. That fool mare thinks she's half rabbit."

Tory turned and gathered her gardening tools quickly. She washed them off at the outside faucet and wiped them on her already fraying jeans. With a grimace she looked down at the thin denim. Next time she would have to buy rugged jeans rather than the fashionable imitations that fell apart under real use.

The thought of buying anything made Tory frown. Money, which she had never had trouble hanging on to before, just kept sliding through her fingers on the Sundance. She had quickly discovered that the tender new plants coming up couldn't be cared for with a shovel or a spade so she had bought gardening tools. While there were plenty of natural fertilizers on the ranch, the gardening book she had bought—another unexpected expense—had mentioned that certain kinds of fertilizers were needed at certain times in the growing cycle. In the end she had bought some commercial fertilizer to be sure that her eager little plants didn't go hungry.

Fertilizer in bags was very expensive. Her anti-inflammation medicine cost even more, but she didn't dare go without it. The repetitious exercises that she did for an hour each night were bad enough without having to cope with a swollen knee as well.

She also needed, and hadn't yet bought, some kind of denim jacket for the cool mornings and nights. The swim club windbreaker she had brought with her just wasn't heavy enough. Then there were the hands' birthdays; it seemed they all came in the summertime. Rather than risk Reever's wrath by taking money out of the kitchen budget, Tory had simply bought candles and funny cards and cake decorations out of her own money. Plus, when she went into Massacre Creek with the hands on ranch business or for pleasure, she refused to let anyone buy her so much as a soda. If everyone ate lunch at the Sunup Café, then so did she, although the food was both relatively expensive and decidedly ordinary.

As a result Tory's bus ticket fund hovered at the halfway mark. No matter how many private vows she made, the fund seemed to stay there. Lately she had expected Reever to ask if she had enough for her bus ticket yet. After all, he hadn't agreed to hire her for all the months she was taking off from diving. He had simply told her that she could cook until she earned enough to buy a bus ticket home. She would just have to pray that Reever wouldn't lose patience with her and kick her off the ranch before she managed to plug the million leaks in her budget.

Besides, Tory didn't really think that Reever would physically throw her off the ranch. To do that he'd have to touch her. And that was something he had not done since the day he had bathed her raw palms so gently and then with equal tenderness had brushed her breasts into aching peaks.

Don't think about it, she told herself fiercely. *You promised yourself that you wouldn't think about it.*

But how do I control the dreams that bring me awake and shivering in the darkness, aching for— Don't think about it!

Tory put the garden tools beneath the sink and began making Jed a thick sandwich using cheese and leftover roast. She moved quickly, anxious to finally begin her riding lessons and to have something to think about besides the hot male sensuality that seethed beneath Reever's cold exterior. She may have attracted him during the forced intimacy of the ride to the ranch, but he had made it very clear since then that he had no use for her as a woman.

City girl. Clumsy. Useless.

Too bad that she still wanted him. Too bad that every time she saw him gently handle an injured animal, or smile and tease Dutch's grandchildren when they visited the Sundance, or drive himself long past the time when another man would have given in to exhaustion, or stand quietly in the evening and look out over the land with love on his face—it was all she could do at those moments not to plead with Reever to look at her again, to see in her the woman of his dreams.

But it hadn't happened. It wasn't going to, either.

Don't think about it.

Tory slammed the screen door and ran out to the corral, clutching Jed's sandwich in one hand and a thermos of coffee in the other. A carrot stuck up out of one hip pocket and her gloves out of the other. She squinted at the brilliant sunlight pouring over the land and wished that she could afford a hat to shield her eyes.

"Here you are, Jed. I brought you some coffee, too."

Jed smiled down at her. "Thanks, Tory. You do spoil us, don't you?"

"I enjoy cooking for the hands," she said honestly. "You're all so appreciative."

"If you'd eaten Cookie's slop, you'd know why. Only thing he could do worth a damn was beans and biscuits. A man can get real tired of beans and biscuits three meals a day." Jed took a big bite out of the sandwich while he waved with his free hand at the corral where a placid old mare with the unlikely name of Twinkletoes stood dozing three-legged in the sun. "She's all yours."

Tory picked up the bridle that Jed had hung over one of the corral posts, ducked it through the cross poles and bridled the mare. While the horse chewed the carrot, Tory brushed her down, smoothed the saddle blanket into place and dragged the heavy saddle off the fence.

"Don't forget the stirrup," mumbled Jed around his last bite of sandwich. "If that chunk of wood comes slamming down on her ribs, even old Twinks here might cut up a bit."

Dutifully Tory hooked the right stirrup over the saddle horn before she swung the bulky saddle onto the mare's fat back. With a grunt and a few muttered words Tory got the saddle into place. Fastening the cinch came next. Twinkletoes knew it, too. Casually the mare took a breath that swelled her barrel to half again its usual size. Tory took a deep breath as well—she didn't like what she was going to do, but there was no other way. She brought her knee up smartly into the mare's barrel. With a disgusted whoosh the mare gave up and let out all the extra air. Quickly Tory tightened the cinch. Twinkletoes stood docilely, unruffled by the whole process.

"Good job," said Jed, sipping at the steaming coffee before setting it aside. "Now gather the reins in your left hand."

Tory did.

"Uh, better try that again," said Jed, walking over until he stood just behind Tory. "If you got on now, by the time you sat in the saddle, the left rein would be laid so hard across her neck that she'd be turning in little circles. Do it like this."

Jed reached over Tory's shoulders with both hands. Holding the reins in his left hand, he raised his hand until it was on the horse's mane just in front of the saddle horn. With his right hand Jed adjusted the reins until they were even on both sides.

"See?"

Tory nodded.

"Now you do it," said Jed, dropping the reins. They fell on either side of the mare's neck and dragged on the ground, for Twinkletoes's bridle didn't come equipped with the single loop of a roping rein.

Tory picked up the reins and did exactly as Jed had done.

"Good. Now," said Jed, putting his arms over Tory's shoulders again, "grab either some mane or the saddle horn in your left hand and—don't drop the reins!—stand by the mare's left shoulder. Take the stirrup in your right hand, turn it toward you, put your left foot in, step up like on a ladder and swing your right leg over the saddle at the same time. If you have to, you can haul yourself up with your right hand on the cantle—that's the back of the saddle that sticks up. Okay?''

Tory had watched the men often enough to have memorized the basic movements. She also had had a lot of practice doing unlikely maneuvers while moving through the air. Being able to use her left hand and foot as stable pivot points was a definite treat after some of the complex dives she had mastered. Besides, she knew that Jed wouldn't tear a piece off her if she didn't get it right the first time.

As though she were getting ready for a dive, Tory mentally reviewed all the moves she had to make. Then she turned the stirrup, stepped into it and swung her leg over the horse's fat rump.

"Hey, that was slick, Tory. You been practicing behind my back?" asked Jed, grinning up at her and casually swatting her leg in congratulations.

"That's just what I was going to ask," Reever said.

Tory froze. She looked from Jed's smiling face to Reever's unsmiling one.

"If I'd known you wanted something to pat and play with," Reever continued, giving Jed a cold stare, "I'd have found you a stray dog."

Jed took his hand off Tory's leg as though he had been burned. He turned to face Reever.

"Thought I told you to ride the east pasture," Reever said, giving Jed no chance to speak.

"I did. A few posts near the slough need work."

"Then get to it."

Although Reever's tone was calm, there was a chill in it that made the words bite like an ice-tipped wind. Jed didn't bother to point out that it was only two hours until dinner and he had already put in a full day. He just jerked his hat into place and left. Tory began to dismount.

"I thought you wanted to learn how to ride," Reever said to her in the same tone that he had used on Jed. "Or was that just an excuse to have Jed's hands all over you?"

"They weren't all—" began Tory hotly, only to be cut off by Reever's slicing words.

"Shut up or get down. But if you get down, you can be damned sure that you'll never learn to ride as long as I'm boss of the Sundance."

Tory closed her eyes and her mouth and took a deep breath. When she opened her eyes, Reever was watching her with an expression she didn't understand, as though he rather than she were being ripped apart. He walked over to the mare and stood looking up at Tory with winter-gray eyes. He was so close that she could feel the vital heat of his body. Except for yanking her out of the henhouse, he hadn't been this close to her in all the weeks since she had cooked her first meal for the Sundance hands.

"The stirrups are too long," Reever said, his voice calm as he stripped off his leather gloves and stuffed them into his hip pocket. He put his hand on Tory's calf and eased her leg away from the stirrup. With quick, clean motions he took up the leather before placing her foot back in the stirrup again. "Rest your weight on the ball of your foot, not the arch. Like this."

It took all of Tory's control not to shiver at the touch of Reever's hands on her leg. She felt chills all the way to her fingertips. She took a shaky breath as he went around the mare's rump and adjusted the right stirrup. When his hands closed over her right leg, she trembled.

Tory watched Reever's hard, sun-browned hands move almost caressingly over her leg as he placed her foot just so in the stirrup. She wanted to ask him if he had to stand so close, if his chest had to brush against her knee, if her leg had to be pressed so intimately down the length of his hard, warm torso as he adjusted the position of her leg in the stirrup. The bare flesh of her ankle felt as though it had been burned, and all he had done was touch her for just an instant with his fingertips.

"Now lift the reins and turn old Twinkletoes to the right."

Tory moved her left hand so that the left rein pressed against the mare's neck. Immediately the horse moved away from the pressure, turning right.

"Walk her around the corral."

Twinkletoes would really rather have stayed put. She let Tory know that be refusing to budge. Tory kicked the broad barrel gently with her heels. The mare didn't notice. Tory nudged her again. The mare stood firm.

"Honey," said Reever dryly, hiding a smile beneath his mustache, "Twinkletoes is so lazy and so fat she can't tell your cute little heels from a fly. If you want to go anywhere, you're going to have to use those long legs for something more than turning Jed on."

Tory pretended it was Reever that she was kicking. Her heels landed with a solid thump. The mare twitched her ears and began walking slowly along the inside of the corral.

"You just keep her headed around the corral while I get Blackjack," said Reever.

In a few minutes Reever returned with Blackjack and a long lead rein that he snapped to Twinkletoes's bit. He saw Tory's mutinous expression and slanted her a hard glance.

"Little girl, I should be shot for letting you anywhere near a stirrup in those flat-heeled city shoes. I'm using the lead rein so that if your clumsiness scares the mare, I'll make sure she can't run away, dragging you behind. If that hurts your tender pride, get off."

Tory looked down at her hands. White showed clearly in the knuckles that grasped the reins. With an effort she forced herself to relax. At least with Reever up on Black-jack he wouldn't be able to touch her as easily.

He could look at her, though. He could make her feel as though he were touching her each time his glance shifted from her hands to her hips to her heels. As they rode side by side, he gave her a running commentary on how she sat wrong, held the reins wrong, held her feet wrong, her hands wrong, her head, her spine, her hips, everything was wrong. The harder she tried, the more clumsy her movements became. Every time his hand brushed over her fingers while he rearranged the reins in her hand, or positioned her leg or her arms correctly, or put his hand on the small of her back to change her posture, it was all she could do not to fall out of the saddle.

Before the ranch was out of sight, Tory decided that she had made a mistake in wanting to learn how to ride. By the time they were over the low rise leading to Wolf Creek, she was fighting not to show her feelings. No matter what she did, it was wrong. No matter how hard she tried, she only became worse. Finally she pulled back on the reins, stopping the mare.

"You win, Reever," Tory said, her voice achingly calm. "I'm convinced I'll never learn to ride."

Reever stopped Blackjack. "City girl, anyone as clumsy as you better learn to take a little criticism."

"Try giving me a *little* sometime," Tory said, fighting to keep her voice even, "and I'll see how I take it." She looked at him, her eyes silently asking for understanding, and added softly, "I'm only awkward around you, Reever."

"Tough. I'm the only teacher you're going to get on the Sundance," he retorted, his voice flat.

Tory closed her eyes for a moment before saying, "Then school's out."

As she spoke, she dismounted from Twinkletoes with a speed that surprised Reever. He came off Blackjack in a single swift motion that placed him only inches from Tory. Instantly she stepped backward, only to bump up against the mare's fat barrel.

"For God's sake," Reever said roughly. "Stop cringing like a whipped pup. I'm not going to touch you."

Being compared to a cringing dog was the last straw for Tory's pride and uncertain temper. "How was I supposed to know that?" she demanded. "You've done nothing but touch me since you came to the corral!"

Reever's face hardened into an expression that made Tory wish desperately that she had followed her original plan for avoiding conflict with him by keeping her mouth shut.

"You sure as hell didn't mind when it was Jed's hands all over you," snarled Reever.

The ice in his voice made Tory shiver. "It's not the same when Jed touches me," she said, her voice so tight that it ached.

"I'll bet. He's young, pretty and has nothing but smiles and soft words for you."

"That's not—" she began hotly.

Reever's hard hand closed over Tory's mouth, sealing in the words with surprising gentleness. He stepped closer, trapping her between his body and that of the docile mare. His thumbs traced the honey line of Tory's eyebrows, touched the outer corners of her faintly tilted eyes and smoothed the hollows beneath her cheekbones before he lifted his hand to caress the trembling bow of her lips.

"Little green-eyed cat," Reever said roughly as he bent down to Tory. "I've wanted to taste you since I looked up and saw you standing on the other side of my desk all those long weeks ago."

Reever's face came closer to Tory until all she could see of the world was the burning clarity of his gray eyes. Then his thick black lashes swept down, concealing the expanding darkness in the center of his eyes as desire exploded through him at just the touch of her breath on his mouth. With the hot, moist tip of his tongue, he traced the sensitive line of her lips until she shivered between his gentle hands.

"Open your mouth," he said, his voice dark, deep. "Don't you want to taste me, too?"

The warm glide of Reever's tongue over the interior softness of Tory's lips made her gasp. Instantly his tongue slid inside her mouth. His heat and salt-sweet taste and slow, caressing tongue sent currents of sensation radiating through her. She forgot to think, to breathe, to do anything except tremble between his hands. Heat claimed her, melting everything, even her bones, until all she could do was cling to his hard forearms when her legs refused to support her any longer.

Reever's hands shifted, no longer gently pinning Tory's head in place for his kiss. There was no more need. She wasn't going to refuse or withdraw from him. He had felt her trembling and the telltale sagging of her weight against his strength, and he knew that desire was claiming her as surely as it had already claimed him. He picked her up and carried her just off the trail to a hollow where grass and wildflowers grew waist-high. Slowly he sank to his knees, lowering Tory into the scented embrace of softly crushed grass and petals.

Tory opened her eyes and took a breath that shook her to her toes. Reever's wide shoulders blocked out the sky as he bent over her, easing his big, hard hands beneath her, arching her up to his hungry mouth. She wanted to say his name, to ask him why he was doing this and to tell him never to stop, but the look on his face froze the words in her throat. His eyes were narrowed, the pupils wide, the rim of iris a hot crystal glitter that made her tremble with answering fire.

Reever's mouth claimed Tory's with a power that made her cling to him. Her hands moved blindly up his arms, across the bunched strength of his shoulders and then swept up beneath his hat, knocking it aside. When she rubbed her palms against his full, thick hair and her fingers found the warmth of his scalp, she gave a husky sound of pleasure. The sound made him shudder against her. His tongue thrust deeply into her mouth, filling her until she arched up to him and her hands clenched in his hair, holding his mouth against hers with all the strength in her young body. She felt as much as heard his harsh groan as he deepened the kiss even more, flattening her beneath him, letting her know the muscular weight of his body all the way to the soles of her feet.

"Am I too heavy for you?" Reever asked, his voice almost rough. "I'd make two of Jed."

The glorious feeling of Reever's body caressing her drove everything from Tory's mind except the need to get even closer to him. She tried to tell him that, but when she opened her eyes, all she could focus on was the sensual line of his lips.

"Reever," she said, and then again, as though the word were being torn from her, "Reever—"

When he heard the passionate breaking of Tory's voice, his hands clenched suddenly and his whole body tightened as though he were being stretched on a rack. Slowly he lowered his head while he watched her eyes. Despite the sensual tension in his body, his lips barely brushed hers, inciting rather than soothing the fires of her hunger. When his tongue slid over the inner softness of her lips, her honey-colored lashes quivered shut as she was overtaken by the sensations coursing through her. She knew nothing but his heat, his touch and the wild pleasure of his mouth slowly, completely, joining hers.

The sweet consummation of the kiss made Tory cry out. The sound was absorbed by Reever as surely as he was absorbing her taste and the touch of her tongue against his. Her response was both innocent and abandoned, unskilled and unaware, hungry and hesitant. For a long moment he moved slowly over her, caressing her with his hard body, claiming her mouth with the same deep rhythms that he wanted to claim her body.

When Reever shifted slightly aside, Tory followed him instinctively, trying to maintain the unexpected, consuming intimacy of the embrace. When he thrust into her mouth again, she whimpered softly and arched against him without realizing it. All she knew was that her breasts were full and her nipples were aching, and when she rubbed against him, it started fires inside her.

"What is it, little girl?" he said, biting her mouth gently, drinking her sudden gasp. "What do you want?"

"Touch me," she breathed in his mouth. "The way you did in the kitchen."

Tory didn't see Reever's triumphant smile or the maddeningly slow movement of his hand toward her breast. Her eyes were closed, and she couldn't breathe for wanting his touch. When his hand stopped just below her breast, she made a breathless sound of protest. She tried to turn, to nestle herself into his palm, but he held her in place. Slowly his hands went from her ribs, to her breastbone, to her collarbone and then back to her ribs. He repeated the caress but came no closer to the aching peaks of her breasts. When he began a third time, she opened her eyes and looked straight into his.

The pale glitter of Reever's eyes as he watched Tory was like lightning beneath the thick arch of his black brows. His face was taut, his lips slightly swollen from his passionate claiming of her mouth. She looked from his face to his teasing fingers. The weight of his hands had pulled the T-shirt tight, outlining her breasts clearly. There was neither loose cloth nor a bra to hide her arousal. The sight of her own nipples nuzzling against the thin cotton made color stain her cheeks.

"Reever?" she whispered.

His thumbs caressed the curves of Tory's breasts but stopped well short of the hungry peaks. "Yes?" he murmured, smiling narrowly as he watched her tighten and rise even more beneath the creamy cotton knit.

"Don't you want to—to touch me?"

"How bad do you want it, little girl?" he asked softly, moving his thumbs slowly, circling her breasts below the nipples. "Bad enough to help me?"

"H-how?"

"Pull up your shirt."

Tory's shock showed in the widening of her green eyes. "I'm not wearing—" Her voice broke as his thumbs barely skimmed the aching nipples.

"I know," Reever said, smiling and watching her helpless response. "Think how it will feel. Your skin and mine, nothing between us but heat and my fingers loving those sweet pink buds until you moan."

Slowly, her hands shaking, feeling awkward and shy and almost afraid, Tory brought up the hem of her T-shirt. The air felt cool against her heated skin as the cloth climbed higher and higher. The material bunched beneath the swell of her breasts and caught on the rigid points of her nipples, making her feel even more awkward. She twisted slowly beneath Reever's pinning weight, trying to remove the T-shirt entirely, only to end up with it tangled thickly under her arms. She twisted again, getting a firmer grip on the stubborn cloth—and then she forgot what she was doing as her whole body tightened in a wild rush. Reever's mouth had claimed her breast just as completely as he had once claimed her lips.

Tory's hands clenched on the T-shirt as Reever's tongue licked hotly at the captive nipple, ringing it in sensual fire. She began to shiver beneath his weight, and her breath came quickly. When he skillfully stroked the sensitive aureole with tongue and teeth, she cried out and wanted him closer, closer, needing the hard suckling of his mouth the way she needed breath itself. She arched against him helplessly, wholly lost. His hand captured her other breast, kneading it, rolling the tight peak between his fingertips, sending more sensual lightning through her body.

The twin assaults made Tory forget everything but the sweet, consuming wildness of Reever's touch. Blindly her hands sought his back and shoulders. She tugged futilely at his shirt, wanting to feel his naked skin against her palms. He shifted aside slightly, giving her access to the snaps on his work shirt, but her hands were shaking so hard that all she did was get tangled helplessly in the blue cloth.

Reever looked down into the innocence of Tory's flushed face. He closed his eyes for an instant, his face tormented. Then with a savage curse he pushed himself away from her. His smoky gray glance swept from her soft, passionately swollen lips to the T-shirt tangled just beneath her arms. Her breasts were full, firm, and their deep pink peaks glistened from the intimate touch of his tongue. Each short, shaky breath she took made her body tremble from her toes to her fingers still caught in the folds of his shirt.

"Did Jed make you want him like this?" Reever asked harshly, watching Tory with cold fire in his eyes.

"I never—wanted him." The words came out in shivering breaths, for Tory could breathe no other way. "Just you. Just *you.*"

Reever looked at her for a long, aching minute, and then he closed his eyes.

"Too bad," he said, yanking Tory's hands free of his shirt and standing up swiftly. "I've spent all the time I can spare on a clumsy city girl."

For a moment Tory lay without moving, stunned. She looked up at Reever's hard face, unable to believe what she had heard. Suddenly she realized that she was half naked, her T-shirt shoved up beneath her arms. She flushed and then went pale. Awkwardly she tried to straighten her T-shirt, but her hands were shaking so hard that she couldn't manage even that. With a cry of shame she rolled over, concealing her naked breasts.

Cursing savagely, Reever bent down and pulled her T-shirt into place, covering the sensual temptation of Tory's tan flesh. "You have enough money for that bus ticket yet?" he asked, his voice harsh.

Tory shook her head, refusing to look at Reever.

"You better get it, little girl. You better get it fast."

Reever mounted his horse and looked down at Tory still lying curled around herself in a nest of grass and wildflowers. He closed his eyes and his hand clenched into a hard fist around the reins.

"Get up," he said quietly. "It's time to go home."

Again she shook her head.

"Tory, don't make me touch you."

Slowly she sat up and looked at him.

Reever's breath came in with a swift, harsh sound as he saw her eyes.

"I know the way back," Tory said, looking through Reever as though he weren't there at all. Her voice was like her eyes, dark, wounded.

"I can't let you ride alone."

"I'll walk."

"It's two miles."

Tory's lips curved in a travesty of a smile. "Walking is one thing even clumsy city girls can do, remember?"

Reever's breath came in with a harsh sound. "Be back by dinner," he said roughly, looking at the soft, honey-colored silk of Tory's hair lifting in the breeze above the vulnerable curve of her neck. "Don't make me come after you. We'll both regret it." He turned Blackjack, then looked back and said, "And stay away from Jed unless you want another lesson. You're too damned hungry to be so innocent. You'd get Jed so hot so fast that he'd hurt you and never even mean to."

"And you're different, right? You're cold so you hurt me—and you mean every bit of it." Tory shuddered with shame at the memory of how she must have looked as she pulled up her T-shirt and clumsily offered herself to Reever. "Go away," she said hoarsely, shaking. "Oh, God, please, go away!"

"Tory—"

Reever's voice was as raw as Tory's, but she didn't hear it. She wasn't even looking at him anymore. She had made him vanish in the only way left to her. She had hugged her legs to her chest until she could rest her forehead on her knees, closing out the world, closing out him.

Tory didn't move or open her eyes, even after the sound of shod hooves faded into silence.

Six

Tory moved awkwardly around the kitchen, trying to favor her right knee without being obvious about it. If Reever saw her limping he would just tear another strip off her for being a clumsy city girl. She couldn't take that right now. She was still too raw from the afternoon. She didn't know what she would do if he turned on her again. She didn't want to know. She had finally admitted that in defiance of common sense and her own usual clear-eyed approach to life, somehow she had managed to fall in love with Reever during the long, sweet, maddening weeks that she had spent side by side with him on the Sundance.

Every day she had spent on the ranch, every hour, every minute, had increased her initial attraction to Reever. She had come to deeply respect his skill and endurance and intelligence. He had taken a ruined ranch and transformed it into a land both productive and beautiful. Although she didn't know enough about ranching to understand all the thousands of hours of sweat and determination the Sundance's transformation had required, she did appreciate the results—fat cattle and sheep, clear streams and lakes, grass everywhere she looked, a land that was obviously cared for with an eye to the future as well as to the bottom line on a budget ledger.

Tory hadn't wanted to admit that her growing love for Reever was why she had been so endlessly vulnerable to his touch. She had told herself that she thought of him as just one more coach she had to please, but she could no longer keep up that pretense. No coach had ever reduced her to tears with a few cold words. No coach had ever made her breath shorten simply by walking past her. No coach had ever set her to secretly dreaming of what it would be like to be a woman with the man she loved, to have a home and children, a chance to build a lifetime of love.

As Tory had walked back to the ranch house, she had finally understood why she hadn't been able to save up enough money to leave the Sundance. She didn't want to leave. She had seen Reever watching her when he thought she wouldn't notice. She had seen and savored the gentleness that lay beneath his harsh exterior, a gentleness he fought against revealing to anyone, especially to her. She had seen him wanting her, and she had kept hoping that if he would only let her close, he would come to love her as she loved him.

Tory bent her head and leaned against the counter until the edge bit deeply into her palms. Silently she raged at herself. *You're a fool, Victoria Wells. You've let yourself in for a world of hurt. You'll never get close to Reever. He won't let you. He knows just the kind of woman he wants, and you are not that woman. The only thing left to do is leave. There sure as hell isn't any point in hanging around, waiting for the judge to explain why you were disqualified from the competition. This is just one of those times you never had a chance.*

City girl. Clumsy. Useless. Too young.

Abruptly Tory shoved away from the counter as though it were her unwelcome thoughts. The incautious movement made pain lance through her right knee. She bit her lip hard, cursing her clumsiness.

She shifted her weight and resumed slicing potatoes into a huge frying pan. Onions followed. She had discovered that the men loved fried potatoes and onions with everything up to and including ice cream. But that wasn't the reason she was cooking them tonight. She had stayed out so long trying to make sense of herself and Reever and her own life that it was nearly dinnertime before she had gotten back. Hamburger steak and fried potatoes were both fast and simple. Even so, dinner would be late. Already the hands were coming in from the range and looking hopefully toward the kitchen.

"Coffee's ready," Tory said, glancing up from the frying pan as Dutch came in. "Dinner in a few minutes."

"Don't hurry," Dutch said, looking curiously at the grass stains visible across the back of Tory's T-shirt.

Jed came in afterward, along with three other hands. The rest were on his heels. Jed, too, saw the grass stains.

"Don't tell me that old Twinkletoes threw you," he said, astonished.

"What?" asked Tory, turning quickly, incautiously, toward Jed. She braced herself on the counter before her right knee could give way beneath the twisting stress.

"The grass stains on your back," Jed explained, picking up the coffeepot and pouring coffee for everyone. "Did you get thrown?"

Tory flushed and nearly dropped the spatula she was using to turn the potatoes. She hadn't even thought that she might have stained her T-shirt rolling around on the grass with Reever. "Yes, I guess you could say I got thrown," she said, her voice raw.

"Hell, Tory," said Jed, setting down the coffeepot and going quickly to the stove. He put his hand on her shoulder. "Don't feel bad. Everyone that rides gets thrown. Even Reever."

"I'd like to congratulate the horse," Tory said, emotion crackling in every word.

The rest of the hands laughed and chimed in, offering comfort and recounting their own experiences "riding air." With her back turned to the table, Tory blindly stirred the potatoes while Dutch finished recounting an unlikely story about Reever riding a mare that was blind, crippled in one leg and the meanest bucker any cowhand had ever straddled. When Dutch told about Reever being unloaded into the manure pile, Tory started smiling, then laughed, shaking her head, not believing a word of it but enjoying the story just the same.

She was still smiling when she turned around with a big dish of steaming fried potatoes and onions in her hand. She hadn't heard Reever come in, but there he was, sitting in his place at the head of the table, watching her with a dark, unreadable expression. Instinctively she flinched from him, only to have her knee protest sharply at the sudden movement. For one awful instant she knew that she was going to fall full-length across the table, scattering potatoes to every corner of the kitchen.

Dutch made a lightning grab and saved the potatoes just as Jed dropped his coffee cup and caught Tory.

"You okay?" asked Jed, ignoring the coffee dripping down his shirt as he set her back on her feet. "You looked like your right leg gave way. Did you hurt it when Twinkletoes dumped you?"

Tory saw only the sudden, harsh look on Reever's face as he loomed over Jed's shoulder. Instantly she remembered Reever's warning about leaving Jed alone.

"I'm fine," she said, pushing away from Jed almost frantically. "Just—" Her voice broke. "Clumsy. Ask Reever. He'll tell you how awfully clumsy I am."

Tory's smile was a travesty of reassurance or humor, but it was the best she could do. She turned away too quickly to see the lines of pain that suddenly bracketed Reever's mouth. In silence she served up the rest of the dinner, not meeting anyone's eyes.

Normally she would have sat down to eat as soon as the food was on the table, but she knew that she couldn't do it that night. She couldn't sit with Reever's long legs not two inches away from hers and his icy gray eyes looking at her and remembering how she had offered herself to him so clumsily that he had been repelled. She couldn't even pretend to push food around on her plate. She knew that she would drop her fork or her coffee cup and further disgrace herself in front of the man she loved.

"I made some cake for dessert. It's in the pie cupboard," Tory said quietly, walking out of the kitchen. "Just leave the dishes on the table when you're finished."

"Aren't you going to eat?" asked Reever. His voice was like his face, aching with the savagery of the restraint that he had imposed on himself.

"I—I ate while I cooked."

"Like hell. You didn't have time. Come back here and eat, Tory," he added almost gently. "You're too thin as it is."

"No, thank you," she said politely, balancing her voice as carefully as she was balancing her body. She hurried around the corner, saying, "I'm really not hungry. Maybe later, after I pack."

Reever ignored the sudden stir as heads turned toward him when the cowhands realized that Tory intended to leave the ranch. One look at Reever's savage expression warned the men that anyone asking a question would probably be invited to drive Tory into Massacre Creek—and stay there.

Tory wasn't sure that she had escaped until she shut her bedroom door behind her. With a shaky sigh she leaned against the heavy wood and bowed her head. To her horror tears began to well silently from her eyes. She wiped impatiently, afraid of being caught crying. After a moment she realized that it didn't matter. There was no father or stepfather or coach to call her a crybaby and no roommate to give her half-sympathetic, half-curious glances. In that, at least, Tory's stay at Sundance had been a success—it had given her a privacy she had never before known.

Ignoring the tears that fell very slowly, Tory peeled off her clothes and pulled on a knee-length green nightshirt. She wouldn't think about Reever and the Sundance and the love that turned in her like a razor with each breath. She couldn't do anything about those things except endure the pain.

Her knee was a different matter. It was within her power to hurt or help her knee. So she ignored her tears, adjusted the elastic support around the knee, sat on the edge of the bed, strapped weights onto her right ankle and began the hour of tedious, repetitious exercises.

She tried not to think as she worked, but it was impossible, just as it was impossible to stop the tears from running down her face in two slow, thin streams.

After so many weeks of exercises, Tory had expected her knee to be much stronger than it was. Even as the doctor had been cautioning her that the healing and rebuilding process would be slow, she had believed that he was wrong. She had believed that if she just worked harder and then harder still, she would be able to achieve her goal of finding a place for herself in the world as an Olympic athlete.

She had believed that it would be the same now as it had always been in the past when she had counted on no one but herself to get what she wanted from life. With her knee as with her diving career, she would ultimately win because of her own discipline and drive, her own ability to work harder than anyone else, to give up more than others would give up, because to her the goal was worth any sacrifice. Anything.

At least, that was how it had worked before. It had to work that way now, too. It simply had to. Nothing had changed. The only person she could lean on was herself.

Counting softly, ticking off exercises and the timed pauses between, Tory worked her knee, ignoring the pain. Eventually the knee would loosen, strengthen, and the pain would stop. Until then she would simply have to work harder.

Tory was softly counting aloud, timing the pause before the final exercise, when the bedroom door opened behind her. She didn't hear it. Nor did she see Reever shut the door behind him and lean against it even as she had. His icy gray eyes saw first her tears, then the white elastic support around her right knee.

"What in God's name have you done to yourself now?" Reever asked roughly.

Tory flinched, then slowly opened her eyes. She saw Reever's face reflected in the dresser mirror and knew that he wasn't going to go away this time if she ignored him.

"Nothing new," she said, closing her eyes again, still counting, hoping against hope that he would leave her alone. She was too vulnerable now, too shaken by the discovery that she was in love with him.

Reever crossed the room and knelt in front of Tory. Her eyes flew open as she felt his hands on her bare leg. He ignored her startled exclamation, just as he ignored her hands futilely trying to push him away. Very gently he peeled down the elastic brace. His breath hissed in when he saw the twin surgical scars bracketing her kneecap. As softly as a sigh, his fingertips tested the slight puffiness of her knee. Then he noticed the weights strapped to her right ankle.

"What the hell are you trying to do to yourself?" Reever asked. His voice was hard, but the hands holding Tory's knee were almost caressing.

"It's called physical therapy," Tory said, trying to pull the elastic support back into place but running into the gentle, immovable barrier of Reever's hands. "I do it every night."

His eyes widened. He looked at the evidence of tears on her face. "Does it hurt like this every night?"

"Depends on how clumsy I've been during the day," Tory said curtly, not wanting to tell Reever that her tears had been as much from unhappiness at discovering herself in love with him as from any pain in her knee.

The lines of Reever's face became more harsh when he heard Tory call herself clumsy, but all he said was, "Have you tried ice?"

"That comes after I finish the last exercise, which you're making impossible."

"I think you've done enough for tonight," Reever said, running his thumbs very delicately over the scars.

Tory shivered at the caress, but her eyes when she met his were unflinching. "No. There's one more exercise I have to do."

Reever looked at Tory, seeing the determination in her that most people overlooked because they noticed only her youth and her lovely, gentle smile. But she wasn't smiling now. Her eyes were older, unwavering. Bleak. He wondered what had happened to make her accept pain without complaint, how she had injured her knee in the first place and what her life had been like before she had arrived on the Sundance and turned his own life upside down.

"What happened?" Reever asked, pulling the brace back into place on Tory's knee.

She wanted to laugh wildly, to release the bitterness of her discovery of a love that he would never return, but she knew she could not. He hadn't asked why she was hurting now. He only wanted to know how she had hurt herself in the past.

"You should have read your cousin's letter," she said.

With that Tory stood up and braced her hands against the bedroom wall. She brought her right heel up to her buttocks and then straightened the leg, repeating the motion in rhythmic sequence. Even though she was careful, she tended to bang her knee or her foot against the wall each time she bent and straightened her leg. Instead of a wall to brace her weight, she needed a fixed, overhead bar that would allow her full freedom to move her leg.

"Here," said Reever, picking Tory up and turning her sideways to him. He extended his long right arm across her breasts, bracing his hand against the wall. "Hold on to me."

She gave him a startled look as she felt currents of awareness course through her from his nearness. Grimly she tore her thoughts away from what she could not have and did as he suggested, bracing herself on his arm.

It was like holding on to a sun-warmed tree branch. He didn't move at all as she flexed her knee and swung her leg with a freedom that hadn't been possible before.

"Better?" he asked quietly, watching her.

"Yes." Tory stared straight ahead, not trusting herself to look at him without giving away everything she was feeling. "Thank you," she added politely.

"What happened, honey?" asked Reever again, his voice as gentle as his hands had been. "I'll call Payton if I have to, but I'd rather you tell me. All of it. Starting when you were a child.''

"Why?" Tory asked flatly. "I'm leaving tomorrow so it doesn't matter."

Reever looked at Tory, all of her, his eyes going from the sun-streaked silk of her hair to her slender, naked feet.

"I have to know," he said simply.

Tory's hands tightened on Reever's arm. Despite his gentle tone, she knew that he was every bit as determined as she had been about finishing her exercises. Reever meant to have his answers one way or another.

"Why?" she asked again, her voice soft, frightened.

"I don't know," Reever admitted, running his left thumb delicately across the slim, tanned fingers holding on to his arm, watching the swift rise of gooseflesh up Tory's arm as she responded helplessly to the caress. "Do you know why you come apart at my touch as though God had made you just for my hands, my mouth, my body?"

"Reever—" Tory's voice broke as he caressed her again. "Don't!"

With a rough word he lifted his fingers from hers. "Talk to me, green eyes. Maybe we'll both find some answers."

For a moment Tory bowed her head, not knowing how to handle the situation. It had always been like that with Reever, from the first time she had seen him. One look, one touch, and finally the kind of love she had never expected to feel. She shivered and her hands gripped the warm, braced power of Reever's arm, remembering when he had told her. *Hold on to me.*

Did she have any choice?

Tory took several deep breaths and let them out slowly, as though she were preparing herself for the most difficult dive of her life.

"I've been swimming since I was six," Tory said as she resumed working her knee, counting off time in her head like a metronome, concentrating on anything and everything but the warm, powerful man standing so close to her, "and diving competitively since I was ten. I'm a better diver than a swimmer. My specialty is platform diving."

Reever saw the jeweled green flash of Tory's sideways glance as she measured his reaction. "Go on," he said.

"Do you know what platform diving is?"

"There's a television in the living room," he said dryly. "We may be so far out in the sticks that the signals arrive a day late, but we do get them eventually."

Tory smiled crookedly. "That's not what I meant. When I say I'm a diver, most people think of springboards, not platforms. Of course, I use the springboard, too, but I like the platform much better."

"Why?"

She hesitated, trying to put into words a choice that had always been instinctive. Like her response to Reever. Instinctive. Irretrievable. "Because every springboard, no matter how carefully it's made to Olympic specifications, is different," she said finally. "The diver is at the mercy of the equipment. It's not that way with a platform. All that gives when you spring is your own body, your knees and your legs. That stays the same, no matter who builds the platform."

Reever glanced sharply at Tory's injured knee.

"Yes," she said, understanding the question he didn't ask. "I can't dive anymore. Not for a while. Not like I used to. And," she closed her eyes as her voice thinned to a whisper, "maybe not ever. I don't know."

For a moment there was silence as Reever thought of all the questions he wanted to ask. He didn't want to hurt Tory any more, but he had to have more answers. He had to.

"Were your parents swimmers?" he asked after a time, wondering how she had been drawn to the sport.

"No."

Reever hesitated. The only other time that Tory had ever mentioned her parents, it hadn't been with pleasure. He could understand that. His own family life hadn't been very pleasant, either.

"Did you always want to dive?" he asked, watching the taut lines of Tory's face as she exercised her knee, feeling himself ache. It seemed as though he had spent his life watching her green eyes darken with pain, pain that he had deliberately caused.

Tory shrugged. "I always had a good time at the pool," she said after a long silence. "Before my parents were divorced, home wasn't a happy place. My mother remarried very quickly. That made it better for her, but not for me. My stepfather—"

Reever felt Tory's hands tighten on his arm, then relax. "You didn't get along," he said.

"We didn't get along," agreed Tory, her voice clipped. "He was very jealous of mother, and I was living proof of the fact that he hadn't been her first lover."

"So you spent a lot of time at the pool," Reever said softly, remembering all the times he had ridden out alone over the land to get away from his father.

"The pool was the only real home I had," Tory said matter-of-factly. "I had a natural talent for diving, but not as much as some of the other kids," she continued. "As long as I worked harder than they did and won more competitions, I was seen as Olympic diving material. I could keep the work-scholarship that made my membership in the swim club possible. I could spend time at the pool instead of at home."

Reever looked at Tory's clean profile, the high forehead and slanting cheekbones, the soft mouth that was now held tightly against the possibility of revealing pain.

"Did you enjoy competing?" he asked, watching her closely, wanting to know, needing it with an intensity that he no longer questioned.

Tory hesitated, wondering how she could explain. She had taken so many things for granted before her injury, before the Sundance, before Reever. As he asked questions, she was finding answers that she hadn't even been aware of before.

"Not really," she admitted finally. "Competition was the price I had to pay for diving. Other kids didn't feel that way. They only truly came alive during a competition when people watched and cheered."

"But not you. It was the diving itself you loved," said Reever, not guessing anymore. Despite Tory's determination, he knew that she was basically too gentle a person to enjoy the kind of cutthroat competition that must have existed as she grew older and had to fight with other divers for footholds on the slippery climb to Olympic glory.

The lines of Tory's face softened as her eyes focused on something that only she could see. "Yes, I love diving. There's nothing like it. When I stand on that platform and gather myself for a dive, nothing else exists. No arguing parents. No unpaid bills. No loneliness. No pain. No exhaustion. Nothing but me and the platform and the pool shimmering below. I used to think that, if I did everything perfectly, I would hang in the air forever, wholly at peace, as graceful as a leaf floating on the wind."

Tory's face changed again, older now. She smiled sadly, lowered her right foot to the floor and let go of Reever's hard, warm forearm. "Thanks, I'm done," she murmured, wincing very slightly as she put her full weight on her right leg.

"Ice?" he asked.

She sank onto the bed, peeled down the elastic knee brace and prodded her knee a good deal less gently than Reever had. "It's not that bad, really. A little swelling, but it won't get in the way of my packing."

Reever's expression darkened. "I'll get you some ice."

Tory started to say that it wasn't necessary, she could get the ice herself or do without it, but Reever was already gone. With a sigh she unstrapped the weights, pulled off the brace and stretched out on the bed. Within a few minutes Reever was back with an ice bag. When she would have sat up again, he put his hand on her shoulder, holding her down gently.

"I'll take care of it," he said. "You look pale."

Tory opened her mouth to tell Reever that it wasn't because of her knee, but caught herself as she realized that he would want to know what was bothering her. He would ask questions, questions that she really didn't want to answer—questions he really wouldn't like the answers to.

In the end she simply moved over to make room for him to sit on the bed, afraid to argue and end the rare moment of peace. She wanted it to continue. She wanted to take from the Sundance more than memories of anger and humiliation. She wanted—too much.

The contrast between Reever's big, warm hand holding her leg and the healing chill of the ice bag was like nothing Tory had ever felt, almost disorienting in its intensity. Her breath came in sharply.

"Does that hurt?" Reever asked quickly, his eyes searching hers.

"No."

He looked at her for a moment longer.

"Really," Tory said, her voice soft. Almost helplessly she added, "You have very gentle hands."

An expression close to pain tightened Reever's face. "How did it happen?" he asked for the third time.

Tory grabbed the question like the lifeline it was. "Ten meters is a long way to fall," she said. "If you land wrong, you can hurt yourself. I wrenched my knee trying to do a triple somersault off the platform. That was a year ago. I came back from the injury, and then one night I slipped in the kitchen at the end of the late shift. I fell with my knee under me at a bad angle, tearing hell out of everything. I had surgery the next day."

"How long ago?" asked Reever, moving the ice bag to the other side of her knee.

"About two months."

Reever went very still. "Do you mean you were going to walk nineteen miles to town three weeks after your knee was operated on and not say a word to me about it?"

Tory smiled sadly. So much for Reever's gentleness; but it had been lovely while it lasted. "People have won marathons three *days* after knee surgery," she said calmly. "Besides, the doctor told me not to baby the knee. Walking is excellent, easy exercise."

"Sure, as long as you're not carrying thirty pounds of badly balanced junk that turns your hands into raw meat," retorted Reever. "And then Billy chasing you over rough country. I should have broken his neck."

Tory's eyes snapped open. The grim lines of Reever's face told her how deep his rage was. Yet when he spoke, it was only to ask another question.

"What did you mean about the late shift in the kitchen? Does the swim club cook for its members?"

She couldn't help laughing. "It wasn't quite that much of a home."

Reever waited impatiently, the flat line of his mouth a silent threat.

Tory closed her eyes again, feeling like crying. It had been so nice not to have Reever angry at her for just a few minutes. "As soon as I turned sixteen," she said tonelessly, "I moved in with three other girls. I got a job at a local coffee shop, first as a waitress, then also as a cook. I worked the late shift because it didn't interfere with my training."

"You worked nights when you were sixteen?" Reever asked roughly, hardly able to believe that her parents had allowed it.

"Believe me, the stove didn't care how old I was."

"God, the drunks must have—" Reever bit off a savage curse as he thought of Tory subjected to an endless string of drunken men trying to sober up for the drive home after the bars had closed.

Tory shrugged. She had hated the drunks, but there had been no help for it. She had needed the job.

"How long do you have to rest the knee before you go back to diving?" Reever tried to make the question calm rather than harsh, but he didn't succeed.

"The doctor said two or three months. If the knee isn't back to full strength by then, chances are it never will be."

Although Tory's voice was calm, Reever could feel the sudden tension in her body when she spoke about her knee. For a moment his hand tightened over the smooth flesh of Tory's upper thigh. Slowly his fingers relaxed, as though by a deliberate effort of will.

"Did you hurt your knee again today?" he asked, his voice strained.

"I zinged it once or twice," Tory said carefully, "but nothing—"

"You little fool!" Reever snarled, not letting her finish. "I would never have let you walk back if I had known that your knee was—"

"Whatever happens to the knee is my fault, not yours," Tory said quickly, cutting across Reever's angry words. "As you've pointed out a hundred times, I'm clumsy."

Reever's mouth flattened beneath the thick black of his mustache. His ice-gray eyes glittered fiercely at her. "You keep pushing, little cat, and you're finally going to make me mad."

"Really?" Tory asked bitterly. "How will I know the difference? Will you wear a sign?"

Reever uncoiled in a single swift movement that ended only when Tory was stretched full-length beneath him, pinned to the bed by his weight. Yet even then he avoided hurting her knee by settling his leg between hers so carefully that she didn't even know what had happened until she took a deep breath and felt him from her shoulders to the soles of her feet.

"You innocent little fool," Reever breathed, his voice ragged as he lowered his mouth to Tory's. "You just don't know when to stop, do you?"

"Reever—"

"Sorry, honey. I warned you. It's too late now."

"No!" Tory said, turning her face aside despite the emotion that had darkened her eyes to emerald. She wanted Reever's embrace with a wildness that frightened her. "I'll come apart when you touch me, and then you'll pull back and cut me to ribbons because I'm so clumsy that I turn you off. I can't take any more of that," she said desperately. "Please, Reever, I promise I'll never talk back to you again. I'll leave first thing in the morning. Please! I can't take any—"

Tory's frantic words ended in a gasp as Reever's teeth fastened lightly on her earlobe. He laughed softly at her response and traced the sensitive rim of her ear with his tongue until she shivered, and he laughed again, triumphantly.

"Sweet little virgin," he whispered, biting her ear with gentle care despite the hunger racing through him with each heartbeat. "I didn't stop making love to you this afternoon because you turned me off. God," he groaned, moving his hips slowly over hers, both easing and increasing the ache of his aroused flesh, "even when I was a kid, I never had a woman turn me on as fast and hard as you do."

Tory's eyes widened and she shivered helplessly as she felt the hard, strong, beautiful length of Reever's body caressing her. "I don't mean to," she said. "I don't even know how to. I just—"

The words ended in a throaty moan as Reever thrust the tip of his tongue into Tory's ear, sending a sunburst of sensation twisting through her.

"Yes," he gritted, feeling Tory's response as though it were his own. "You just come apart when I touch you, that's all. Knowing you're a virgin, knowing you would melt and run for me like hot, wild honey—" He stifled a groan. "It's killing me, little one. I should be shot for even kissing you, but I want to do more than just this. I want to slide that nightshirt up your beautiful, innocent body and let you feel my hands and mouth everywhere, all over you, every hot, sweet bit of you. Oh, God, green eyes, you can't even imagine the things I want to do to that untouched body!"

Reever heard the tiny, wild sound Tory made, felt the involuntary arching of her body beneath him as his words set fire to her.

"Don't," he said hoarsely, holding her still, forcing himself not to stroke her body with his own. "I can't sleep at night for wanting you, but I won't take your innocence and give you only experience in return. A girl should at least hear 'I love you' from her first man, whether it's true or not—but I can't lie to you that way, Tory. That's why I've done everything but beat you with a whip to drive you away from the Sundance. From me."

With an aching sound Reever brushed his open mouth over Tory's trembling lips, tasting her with tiny touches of his tongue even while he spoke. "I sat on that damned ridge this afternoon and I watched you through the glasses and I hated myself for hurting you like that. I watched you walk all the way back to the ranch, and I wanted you until I felt like knives were turning in me."

Reever's breath washed warmly over Tory's lips as his tongue dipped lightly into the corners of her mouth. "It tore me apart to watch, but I had to know you were all right. I wanted to go to you, help you, and I knew if I went any closer, I would take you down into that soft grass and love you until you didn't know where you were, who you were, until you could touch me and not know whether it was my skin or yours you were feeling, my body or yours, because we would be so deep in each other that it would be like dying and being born all over again. It's never been like that for me with a woman, but I know it would be like that with you. I know it, and it's tearing me apart."

The small, involuntary sound Tory made ate at Reever's control.

"Oh, God, don't," he said raggedly, caressing Tory's face with his lips, his tongue, his teeth. "Don't move. Don't make a sound. I thought I could trust myself, but I can't. Not with you. And I'll hate myself if I take you. You deserve a gold ring and sacred vows. I can't give you that, sweet little city girl. We're all wrong for each other that way. But I couldn't let you leave tomorrow thinking I was cruel. Every time I had to hurt you, I bled. I'm still bleeding."

A shudder went the length of Tory's body. She closed her eyes, releasing a bright shimmer of tears. She remembered with terrible clarity what Reever had told her—when he married a woman, she would be just that, a woman. Not a young, clumsy city girl.

The thought was a razor slicing through Tory, making her bleed in ways she couldn't name. She knew that she would never love another man as she loved Ethan Reever. She loved him, and she was leaving him. She would never know what it felt like to give herself to the man she loved.

"Have I ever asked you for anything but a job?" Tory asked with aching quiet, her voice shaking, her tear-bright gaze holding Reever's. "This afternoon, did I push your hands away and say that you couldn't touch me until you gave me a gold ring and told me that you'd love me until you died?"

"No. But you should have," Reever said tightly. "You should have made me promise you the moon. I would have. I wanted you so bad I was all but blind."

"Do you think that's why I'm still a virgin?" Tory asked suddenly, as anger curled along her nerves. "Is that how little you think of me? Do you believe that I want to drive a man out of his mind with desire and then hold out on him until I trap him into marriage? You're wrong, Ethan Reever," she said harshly, the words tumbling out in a heedless rush, driven by the three words she could not say: I love you. "I'm a virgin because I've never lov—I've never *wanted* a man enough to let him undress me and touch me until I can't breathe for wanting more. I've never wanted a man to know my body in ways that even I don't, to be moving inside me, a part of me. I'm nearly twenty-one years old, and I've never wanted a man in any way at all. Until you."

Reever's eyes narrowed until they were slits of glittering ice. "Haven't you been listening? I have nothing to give you but passion."

"Why should I want anything more?" Tory whispered raggedly, touching Reever's cheek with her fingertips. "I never expected to have even passion from you. I want you to be my first. I want you to be the one to teach me. I want it all to happen with you, even the things I can't imagine. Especially those things, Reever.''

"Tory—" groaned Reever, fighting for control.

"No," she said quickly, interrupting him by putting her fingers over the lips that were barely half an inch from hers. "Listen to me, Reever. I know myself. I know that I'll never—want—another man the way I want you. Don't refuse me. I promise I won't ask or expect anything else from you except your hands, your mouth, your body teaching me how to worship you."

Tory trembled as Reever brushed aside her fingers and kissed her so deeply that she couldn't breathe. After a long, long time he lifted his head and spoke in a shaking voice.

"You sweet, sweet little fool, don't you know what it does to a man to be told that he's wanted like that?"

"What does it do?" she whispered huskily. "Teach me, Reever. Teach me everything."

Seven

Reever closed his eyes and didn't breathe, didn't speak. From his clenched fists to the soles of his feet, his body was as hard as steel, as motionless, and his expression was almost agonized. Tory felt tears scald down her cheeks as the certainty grew in her that he was going to reject her again.

The thought made Tory want to cry out in protest, pleading with Reever not to turn away from the woman who loved him. Yet even as the words crowded her tongue, she knew that she must not say them. If she said *I love you,* she would drive Reever away from her. He would simply take her words as proof that she was too immature to give herself physically to a man without the fiction of love between them.

But it wasn't a fiction. She did love him. She hadn't wanted to fall in love with any man, had never really expected to, but she had come to love Reever just the same. Deeply. Passionately. That was why she hadn't been able to save enough money to leave the Sundance. She didn't want to leave. She had seen Reever watching her, wanting her, and she had kept hoping that he might be falling in love with her as she had fallen in love with him—one day at a time, one glance, one look, one touch.

It hadn't happened that way after all. She had fallen alone. She was still falling.

Tory shut her eyes and fought to control herself in the face of Reever's rejection, but it was impossible. She couldn't even turn away, for she was still pinned to the bed by the weight of his big body. Helplessly she began to cry, her body shaking with tearing, silent emotion.

Reever rolled aside and gathered Tory into his arms, holding her very gently.

"Don't be frightened," he murmured, stroking her back slowly, nuzzling her mouth with a tenderness that made her shiver. "I want you until I'm crazy with it, but I won't hurt you. I swear it. I'll tease and love that sweet body until you're shaking and wild, and when I finally take you..." Reever groaned and his hands tightened on her soft skin. "Oh, God, little cat, when I take you, it will be like falling into the sun. You can't feel pain when you're burning alive with pleasure."

Reever looked down into Tory's huge, tear-bright eyes. "I know it's a lot to ask for after the last few weeks," he said huskily, "but will you trust me not to hurt you?"

Tory tried to speak through trembling lips, couldn't, and nodded instead. When she could trust herself not to blurt out her love, she tried to ask him to be patient with her, not to cut her up for being clumsy. At first all she could say was his name, the word a question trembling on her lips. "R-Reever?"

"Yes?" he breathed, kissing the corner of Tory's mouth with exquisite care.

"I'll try not to—to be clumsy, but please don't—"

"Hush, little one," Reever said, licking up Tory's painful words with the warm tip of his tongue. "You aren't clumsy at all. You're as graceful as sunlight on water. Watching you used to make me ache until I felt like something was tying my guts in knots. I'd lash out at you, trying to keep you away, trying to make you hate me instead of want me, and then I'd have to watch the light in your eyes die as you turned away from me." He shuddered. "Innocent little green eyes," he whispered, sipping at Tory's mouth with tiny touches of his lips and tongue. "I've never seen anything half as graceful and lovely as you. Remember that. Forget the lies and remember that truth because it's the only one that matters."

Reever fitted his mouth exactly to Tory's trembling lips, cherishing her with a gentleness that brought more tears to her eyes. He rocked his head slowly back and forth, changing the feeling of the kiss with each small movement, sensitizing her lips until she felt as though she were on fire. She wanted to put her arms around him, to bury her fingers in his hair and hold his teasing, beautiful mouth against hers. But despite his assurances she was afraid that he would think her clumsy whether he said it aloud or not.

"So soft," Reever murmured, biting Tory's lips with tender care. "And even softer inside. Open for me, honey. I've been driving myself crazy remembering how sweet you taste, how soft you are, how warm and giving."

"Reever," she whispered.

"More," he said, nuzzling her mouth. "I want to see you ready for me, waiting. I have to know you want my mouth."

With a shudder Tory parted her lips. She watched Reever's eyes widen and darken to a smoky gray. She looked at the sensual lines of his mouth and remembered how it had felt when he had kissed her so deeply that she hadn't been able to breathe. She wanted that again. She wanted the hard, complete claiming of his mouth, the taste and scent of him filling her until she couldn't tell where she ended and he began.

"What are you thinking?" Reever asked huskily, watching Tory's eyes and her parted lips, wanting to taste and feel her tongue sliding over his.

"Your mouth," she said, her voice trembling. "It isn't fair that a man should have such a beautiful mouth. And what you can do with it—" Her breath came in sharply with another burst of memories, of the heat and intimacy of him cherishing her breasts. "That isn't fair, either."

Reever's laugh was low and very male, a sound both sensual and triumphant. "Do you want my mouth?" he asked, nuzzling her teasingly.

"Yes," Tory breathed, watching him.

"How? Like this?"

The gentle torment of his lips and tongue continued, but other than tracing the line of her teeth, he made no move to claim the parted lips that she offered him. Tory put her arms around Reever's neck and tried to pull him closer. He was too strong. No matter how she tugged, he kept on teasing her, pinning her gently to the bed, not allowing her to come closer.

"Reever," said Tory urgently.

As she said his name, he took her mouth with a hot, slow movement of his tongue, teasing and caressing her even as he absorbed her into himself. She shivered uncontrollably at the sweet consummation, giving him even more of herself as she sought to taste more of him. The impact of the kiss left her disoriented, shivering, able only to hold on to him as the rest of the world fell away.

Gradually she began to move her tongue as he did, caressing him as he was caressing her. He made a thick sound of pleasure and deepened the kiss even more, exploring every dark, soft curve of her mouth until the kiss became an act of intimacy that made her feel both ravished and cherished. When he lifted his mouth, she tried to follow him, wanting more of him, trembling with her wanting.

"Easy, little cat," Reever said, his voice ragged. He looked down at the sweet young mouth blindly seeking his and didn't know whether to swear or shout with triumph. "So innocent. So hot. *God*."

Tory's eyes half opened, shadowed by a thick fringe of lashes. She ran the tip of her tongue over her lips, and her eyes widened in surprise. "I taste like you," she whispered.

With a low groan Reever arched his hips into Tory, trying to ease the pain that was also pleasure.

"Don't say things like that," he grated. Then he saw her face change, passion draining into hurt. "Tory," he said, kissing her swiftly, repeatedly, calling her name between kisses. "I didn't mean it like that. I'm trying to go slow with you, but you're so damned sexy and giving and honest that I—" He took a shuddering breath and slowly lowered his hips into the soft cradle of her thighs. "Tell me again," he whispered thickly, licking her lips with hot touches of his tongue.

"Reever—"

"Tell me, Tory. Feel what it does to me."

Hesitantly his tongue touched her lips. She shivered as the tip of his tongue met hers. "I was wrong," she whispered. "We taste like each other."

The words ended in a tiny cry as she felt his powerful body tighten like a drawn bow. The hard length of his arousal caressed her intimately, separated from her only by his clothes and the thin satin smoothness of her underwear.

"You're right, little cat," Reever groaned. "I taste like you and you taste like me." He bit Tory's mouth gently, hungrily. "Say whatever you like. Say it whenever you like. I want to hear you. I want everything you think, everything you feel, everything you are. I want—" Reever laughed shortly and shook his head. "The things I want would shock you now. But not in a while. In a while you'll want everything I have, all of it, all the way, and you'll want it until you scream."

Tory's fingers flexed on Reever's shoulders as she shivered at the hot words flowing over her, making her burn. She watched his mouth hungrily. She loved the feel of it, hard and resilient, warm and skilled, teaching her things about hunger and satisfaction that she had never suspected could be learned from a kiss.

Hesitantly she ran her fingertips over his lips, tracing their clean outline until she touched his teeth. The difference between his lips and the small serrations of his teeth fascinated her. She ran her fingertip over him again. When the tip of his tongue licked hotly over her, she made a small sound of surprise and pleasure. She dipped into his mouth again and then again, enjoying his changing textures, touching him slowly, rhythmically, not knowing that her whole body was moving beneath his in the same slow rhythms of discovery.

Reever took as much of the sweet torment as he could before he turned his head away sharply, fighting for control. He felt Tory flinch and snatch back her hand.

"Tory—" he began, trying to explain.

"No," she said in a raw voice, covering his mouth with her hand. "Don't say it. Please, don't say it. I know I'm clumsy. I'm sorry, it's just that I've never done this before. I don't know what I should or shouldn't do."

Reever saw the legacy of pain in Tory's eyes, pain echoing from his cruel remarks ever since he had first seen her, wanted her like he had never wanted another woman and known that he shouldn't even kiss her.

And the worst of it was realizing that he had savaged her more deeply than he had ever intended because he hadn't really believed that he could hurt her at all. Not like this, her humiliation strong enough to taste.

The realization that Tory had no defenses against him shocked Reever even as it humbled him. He felt the same with her and had from the first moment. No defenses. Just a need and a fire that transformed him, giving him a strength and gentleness that he had never dreamed was possible for him.

"Tory," Reever murmured, kissing her softly with each breath, each instant. "My sweet, sensuous little virgin. I accused you of being clumsy because I was afraid to have you know what your grace did to me. You made me—burn. No other woman has ever done that to me. A look. A smile. A word. You didn't have to touch me. All you had to do was be there and my body—changed. Oh, God, honey. I got so hard I thought I'd die unless I undressed you and eased into that slender, perfect body. I almost took you the first time I saw you. And then on the ride back to the ranch, all I wanted to do was turn you around on Blackjack and slide you down over me and—"

With a shudder Reever stopped the reckless words, afraid that he would frighten Tory. "You are not clumsy," he said, biting off each word. "I pulled away just now because your sweet, sexy little moves almost made me lose control. I want you so much I'm afraid I'll hurt you."

Tory's eyes widened as she saw the truth written in every hard line of Reever's face. She believed him. She believed that he wanted her so much it was an agony inside him.

"Take me," Tory whispered, holding his face with trembling hands. "Take me where you're touching me now, where you're making me ache. Please, Reever. You can't hurt me more than I already hurt right now."

A few moments ago Reever would have taken her right there, ending his torment within her soft, willing body. But now he knew that there was no end to her vulnerability to him. Knowing that, he found the strength to be gentle.

"I'll take you," he promised, kissing her slowly, joining their mouths as perfectly as he knew he would join their bodies. "Eventually. But I want to know you first. And I want you to know me."

Reever's hand went from Tory's back to her ribs. He hesitated there, savoring her suddenly taut body and the sound of breath wedging in her throat. Smiling, he watched her nipples harden until they thrust against the soft cotton nightshirt in silent pleading for his caress.

"They remember me, don't they?" he murmured. "Which do you want first, honey—my hands or my mouth?"

Tory blushed at Reever's sensual teasing even as her back arched reflexively, bringing her breasts closer to his mouth. He saw her helpless reaction and smiled.

"Wild little innocent. So sweet. God, I could die finding out how sweet you are, and how wild."

Reever nuzzled one of Tory's breasts, drawing a ragged sound from her. He smiled again and slowly caught her erect nipple between his lips, tugging rhythmically as he drew her deeper and deeper into his mouth, listening to her tiny cries. After a long time he lifted his head and looked down at her breast. Wet from his mouth, the cotton was nearly transparent. It clung faithfully to her taut nipple. The rose-tipped breast made a warm, inviting contrast with the cloth clinging to it.

Groaning softly, Reever kissed the sweet peak once more before he turned his head aside and found her other breast.

He suckled her languidly, deeply, hotly, wringing soft cries from her as she twisted in slow motion against him, seeking release for the tension coiling more and more tightly within her with each movement of his mouth. After a long, long time he released her, only to bite lightly again and again at the sensitive nipple until he felt the unmistakable shudder of true arousal take her slender body.

Reever's hands moved to the hem of Tory's nightshirt, which had been drawn up above her hips by her movements. He brought the shirt up to Tory's breasts a little at a time, nuzzling and teasing her with his mouth every bit of the way until he found her nipples again. They were still aroused, still needing him. As his warm mouth closed over one, she shuddered and unconsciously rocked her hips against his as pleasure expanded through her.

The movement tore a low groan from him. His mouth changed, caressing her with a lover's fierce demand. He felt the fire rip through her, felt her body arch beneath his, felt her intimate heat penetrating the heavy cloth of his jeans as he stilled her wild movements by letting his weight sink into her, pinning her to the bed.

"Easy, little one, easy," Reever said again and again, gentling Tory even as he fought his own violent need to give her what she was silently, innocently, begging him for.

"Reever?" Tory's question ended in a moan as his teeth closed with exquisite delicacy on her breast.

"Am I too heavy for you?" he asked, tugging at her, watching ripples of sensation race over her skin.

Tory's only answer was a husky sound as she eased her legs farther apart, trying to get even closer to Reever. The innocent sensuality of the movement made him groan. His hand swept down her body to her thigh as he attempted to hold her still. He saw her eyes widen in surprise when his palm brushed over the apex of her thighs. He knew in that instant that she had never been touched, never known a man's hand caressing the softness of her inner thighs, never known the seeking and finding and caressing of even softer flesh.

"Oh, God, little one," Reever said huskily, biting at the shadow dimple of Tory's navel, feeling the wild response coursing through her. "I've got to touch you. It may shock you at first, but when you get past that, you'll know you want it as much as I do. You'll know that you belong to me everywhere, no matter how secret."

Reever's hand smoothed down Tory's body again. The heel of his palm pressed against the sensitive feminine nub hidden beneath her tangled hair, and then his caress moved on to the smoothness of her inner thighs. He watched her face, not wanting to frighten her by a touch that was too new, too intimate for her to accept. He sensed the instant of her uneasiness and hesitation as his hand settled between her thighs. His fingertips stroked delicately over even more delicate flesh.

"I won't hurt you," Reever promised. His voice broke as he looked down at Tory's flushed cheeks and passionate mouth. "You don't know what you do to me," he said hoarsely. "You make me want—everything. Look at me, sweet virgin. Tell me if I frighten you."

Tory's eyes opened, revealing a deep green rim around pupils dilated by sensual response. Reever's breath came in with a hiss as he saw the evidence of her arousal. He felt as though he were being licked by fire. His fingertips slid over the satin triangle of her underwear, barely touching her, yet she trembled violently. His hand caressed her thighs reassuringly as he bent and kissed her breasts and then her lips, tasting her with a consuming sensuality that made her shiver and moan.

"It's all right," he murmured. "I won't do anything you aren't ready for."

"I feel so—strange," she whispered, staring into his eyes.

"Frightened?" he asked softly.

Tory shook her head. "It's just that—I thought I knew everything about my own body. But I didn't. I didn't know that you could touch me and I would feel it all over, everywhere. Even—"

"Even?" he asked.

"Inside," she whispered, "where no one has ever touched me."

Reever's whole body tightened, but when he spoke, his tone was very gentle.

"I'm going to touch you there," he said, bending and kissing Tory's mouth. Gently his fingers smoothed over the thin, sheer cloth separating him from her hidden warmth. When she began to tremble, he lifted his head, looking at her. "Let me," he said quietly. "I won't hurt you. I'll be so gentle that all you'll feel will be pleasure. Just let yourself respond as honestly as you responded when I loved your breasts until you moaned. Remember how it felt for you then," he said, his voice husky, "because that's just the smallest beginning of the pleasure I can bring you."

While Reever spoke, his hand moved caressingly between Tory's thighs. At first she lay stiffly, but after a few moments she relaxed and let the shimmering pleasure of his touch spread through her. Without realizing it, she sighed and shifted, opening her legs a bit more. She wondered why his eyes narrowed then as he smiled down at her, but the sweetness of his touch drove all thoughts from her mind.

Slowly he bent over and kissed her navel, letting her feel his teeth and tongue until her hips lifted with the involuntary sensual response he had been waiting for. At that instant he slid the sheer panties down her legs with a sweep of his hand. Any objections she might have had were lost when his mouth locked over hers, and he consumed her with strokes of his tongue that made her moan and move sinuously, slowly.

By the time Tory realized that the wild sensations shivering through her were coming from Reever's palm moving slowly between her legs, it was too late to be shy or frightened. She could only do as he asked, as he urged, opening herself to his touch, watching his eyes darken with the same wild desire that was shaking her.

Delicately, gently, he traced her layered softness with his fingertips, watching her eyes change as she understood what was happening.

"Yes," Reever whispered, teasing the tiny, sensitive bud hidden in Tory's softness. "You can feel what it will be like, can't you? You can feel us coming closer and closer to the instant when you'll give yourself to me."

Tory's breath came in with a moan as she felt Reever begin to deepen the caress with a tenderness that made her forget to be afraid. She watched his eyes through half-closed lids while he gently took more and more of her secret softness, and she felt as though he were unraveling her bones. She moaned again, watching him, unconsciously moving in counterpart to his touch, wanting more of him.

"You're like a dancer, all grace and fire," Reever said, smiling, holding Tory's glance as his touch slid more deeply into her and she gasped with pleasure and surprise. "Yes," he grated, "let me know how much you like it. Let me know how—" His words ended in a groan as she melted at his touch. He watched her eyes, saw her surprise consumed by another burst of pleasure when he caressed her intimately. "You're so hot, so soft, so perfect," he breathed, bending down to her. "You make me want to come apart right here, right now, with you watching me." He shuddered and took her mouth with a thrust of his tongue. "Little virgin," he said huskily, biting her neck and shoulder with barely leashed hunger. "But not for long."

Reever's hand moved hotly, intimately, and Tory cried out again, melting again. His smile was a savage mixture of pleasure and the pain of not taking her. Tory saw the smile and felt lightning race through her, a sensual hunger that he was focusing with each searching caress. She reached for him, needing the consummation of his mouth, needing to feel his weight over her, moving, and her own body moving in return, needing something she had never known and could not even describe.

"Reever, I want—" Tory's voice broke as pleasure radiated through her at his touch, a slow, bursting heat that made her moan.

"What?" he murmured, slowly releasing her, letting his hand slide up to her navel, teasing the dimple with his warm, damp fingertip. "What do you want?"

Tory's hands closed on Reever's shirt as she tried to bring him closer. The metal snaps gave way in a ripple of sound. For the first time she felt his naked skin against her palms. She made a sound of satisfaction and discovery, excited by his heat and the sensual tension that brought each of his powerful muscles into hard relief. The wedge of blue-black hair enticed her, caressing the sensitive skin between her fingers as she rubbed against him.

"Tory—"

"No," she said huskily, flexing her fingers until her nails dug in lightly and he groaned. "Don't make me stop. You feel so good, Reever. Or don't you—don't you want me to touch you?"

His laugh was a ragged sound that was torn from him. She knew the answer to her question even before he spoke because he was moving with her touch, twisting slowly, increasing the pressure of her fingers exploring his chest.

"I want your hands all over me," Reever said, his voice as deep and ragged as his laughter had been. His eyes sought and held Tory's. "But if I let you undress me, touch me, your time as a virgin will be over. I don't want it to end that quickly. It's only going to happen for you once, green eyes. That's worth waiting for." He shuddered as he felt her nails skim over his nipples. "Besides, if you see how much I want you, it may just scare the hell out of you."

Reever tried to lighten his words with a smile, but he couldn't. Just the thought of Tory turning away from him in fear made him want to take her right there, right now, before she could change her mind.

Tory heard the truth and buried fear in Reever's words and wondered how she could tell him that she was no longer afraid. All the words she could think of began and ended in *I love you,* and those were the words she must not speak. Her hands slid down his chest to his hard waist. The involuntary, sudden movement of his abdomen surprised her until she remembered that she, too, had responded like that at the first touch of his fingers sliding down her body. And it had been pleasure, not surprise or distaste that had moved her.

"Did you like that?" she asked softly, watching the smoky glitter of his eyes.

"Yes," Reever said, his voice almost harsh.

"And this?"

Tory's hands slid lower, seeking and finding the hard length of him pressing stiffly against the confinement of his jeans. Reever's hips moved involuntarily, and a groan was ripped from him at the first sweet touch of her hands on his aching male flesh.

"Oh, God," he gritted, closing his eyes and shuddering heavily. He put his hands over Tory's as though to push her away, but he could not. His need was too great. He pressed her hands harder against him and moved slowly, shaking with hunger and pleasure.

Then Reever opened his eyes and saw Tory watching him, sharing his pleasure as he had shared hers. For a moment he thought he would lose control. Only his determination and deep need to be inside her allowed him to drag himself back from the brink. The realization surprised him. With other women it hadn't particularly mattered to him how he found satisfaction. Yet it mattered with Tory. He didn't know why; he only knew that it did. It was a truth that was even stronger than his blazing sexual need.

Gently Reever smoothed Tory's hands up the length of his body until he could bite her palms and fingertips with barely controlled force, wringing cries of sensual surprise and response from her trembling mouth.

"I think you've made your point," Reever said, giving Tory a smile that made her heart turn over. "You may be a virgin, but you won't faint or run screaming if you see me naked."

Reever kicked off his boots and stood up, making no attempt to conceal himself from Tory's curious eyes. He watched her face as he took off his shirt and tossed it aside. The sound of her indrawn breath was like a caress.

"I'd think you'd be used to seeing half-naked men," Reever said, smiling at her, his hands resting on his belt buckle. "Or do they swim in T-shirts where you come from?"

Tory smiled without looking away from Reever's powerful shoulders and the sleek black pelt curling down to his belt buckle. "Oh, I'm used to seeing men in a scrap of cloth that isn't even worth mentioning," she agreed. "But they shave all their body hair to cut down on drag in the water. And even if they didn't shave..." Tory shivered as her glance moved over Reever like a caress. "They aren't you, Reever. No man is. No man ever will be."

The words sank into Reever like sweet tiny claws, bringing a violent surge of desire. He wondered again how anyone as honestly passionate as Tory had managed to stay out of a man's bed for so many years—and then he remembered what she had told him: *It was easy. I hadn't met you.*

Watching Tory, Reever unbuckled his belt, unfastened his jeans and pulled off all his clothes with a few swift motions. As her glance traveled down his body, he saw her curiosity, her approval and then her surprise at the extent of his desire for her. He realized that, even though she had spent most of her life around nearly naked men, she was totally unused to seeing a man who was fully aroused.

"It's too late to change your mind and run screaming," said Reever, lying down next to Tory again, touching her with a hand that trembled.

"How about fainting?" she asked, her voice shaking, breathless. "Is that still an option?"

"Don't be afraid, little cat," Reever said, kissing Tory gently despite the violence of his own need. "I know it seems impossible to you right now, but you'll fit me like a satin glove, all hot and smooth and close."

Reever's hand kneaded gently down Tory's body until he found and caressed again the softness hidden between her legs. As his fingers teased her feminine bud, she shivered and melted again with a tiny gasp.

"All of a man's changes are obvious," he murmured, nuzzling against her breast. "Yours are subtle, almost secret, until I touch what's hidden and feel how very soft you've become for me. If you would touch yourself, you would feel how you've changed for me. You can hold me inside you now and have only pleasure, not pain."

Reever saw Tory's helpless blush at the thought of touching herself and he smiled. "Then you'll just have to take my word for it, won't you?"

Her only answer was a ragged intake of her breath as his hand slid caressingly between her thighs. His fingertips tormented her so delicately that after a few moments she forgot to be nervous or shy. Involuntarily her leg flexed as she shifted in response to his teasing, maddening, incredibly arousing touch. As he found once again her hidden heat and need, her eyelids fluttered shut and she lost herself in the sensations he drew from her.

Tory moved her hips gently, sinuously, beneath Reever's caress as she opened to him completely. His eyes darkened and narrowed at her wordless, unconscious invitation. Seeing her so vulnerable, so trusting, so generous with her virginal body made him ache to bend down to her and tease her softness with his tongue, to know every shivering bit of her in an intimacy that he had never shared with another woman. With a groan he forced himself to look away from her secrets lying open to his touch.

But Reever could not wholly refuse the invitation that Tory had so innocently and hotly given to him. Gently he covered her body with his own, easing himself into the cradle of her thighs. Her eyes flew open even as her body tightened.

"It's all right," Reever breathed, brushing Tory's lips with his open mouth, biting at her gently. "I won't take you by surprise, little one. You're going to have your eyes wide open—and so am I." He shuddered as his violently aroused flesh nudged against Tory's moist, vulnerable core. "I'm going to enjoy every instant of you every way I can. I've never wanted a woman like this. I want all of you, Tory. I want to watch your face as you change from virgin to lover with a single stroke of my body.''

Tory shivered and moved beneath Reever while he teased her with his hands and the hungry, hot length of him rubbing over her. Always he stopped at the edge of taking her, barely penetrating, giving her just enough of himself to make her wild to have more. Finally she gave a ragged cry and arched herself against him, instinctively trying to capture and hold him within herself.

As Tory's hands gripped the hard muscles of Reever's buttocks, he jerked reflexively, sliding more deeply into her, stopping just short of the irrevocable instant when he would transform her. She twisted wildly as she tried to evade his restraint. Her body was like his, hot, shining with a mist of desire that increased the sensitivity of skin rubbing over skin. She twisted again, blindly seeking what he had prepared her for. His arm wrapped powerfully around her hips, stilling her movements. With a thick sound he bent and took her mouth, pinning her completely, letting the shaking wildness pass.

"Look at me," Reever said in a gritty voice. "Tell me how you want me. Slow or fast, tender or wild, whatever you want. I want it to be so good for you. I want it to be the best you'll ever have."

Tory's eyes, almost black with desire, opened. "How should it be? How is it best?" she asked, her voice trembling.

"Hot. Deep. Forever."

Tory's nails dug into the rigid muscles of Reever's body as the words burst through her. "Yes," she whispered, arching helplessly against him, repeating the word with each rapid breath she took.

Tory felt Reever going deeper into her and shivered as his heat became part of her. When he reached the fragile barrier he stopped. She opened her eyes, knowing that he was watching her, waiting for her.

"Am I hurting you?" he asked, and his whole body trembled with the effort of controlling his own violent need. "Tell me, green eyes. I'll never forgive myself if I hurt you."

The contrast between Reever's gentle words and the savage restraint of his body undid Tory. She shivered repeatedly as fire raced through her. All she could say was his name, but he felt the wild heat of her melting around him and knew that at that instant she could feel only pleasure. He thrust into her, sweeping aside the barrier, sheathing himself deeply in her welcoming softness. He saw her eyes widen with realization and heard her breath sigh out in a moan of sensual pleasure that was also his name.

"You're mine now, little cat," Reever gritted, bending to take Tory's mouth as completely as he had taken her body. "Oh, God, you feel good, hot and sweet and deep."

Reever's tongue thrust and withdrew slowly, matching his other movements within Tory. She trembled and washed over him in hot waves of pleasure. She sought to take more of him and give more of herself as she reached instinctively for the ecstasy that shimmered just beyond reach.

When Reever felt Tory twist beneath him, seeking him fully, his control slipped. He arched into her, filling her, wanting the same release that she was reaching for. Her tiny, wild cry ripped through him. Desperately he forced himself to lie still, afraid that his instant of uncontrolled need had hurt her. But when he would have withdrawn slightly in order to spare her, she grasped his hips, trying to get closer to him.

"Do you want more of me, little one? Is that it?" Reever asked, biting Tory's nipple with sensual restraint, shuddering when pleasure burst through her and melted over him in the same hot instant. "Wrap your legs around my hips," he urged huskily. "If it hurts, I'll—" His voice broke as she shifted, wrapping around him, taking all of him, and telling him of her pleasure with every movement of her slender body. He rocked slowly against her, feeling currents of fire gather with each hot, sliding instant. "Am I—hurting you?" he asked, barely able to breathe, moving in tight, tiny circles against her, inflaming both of them.

Tory's whole body stiffened suddenly as her breath unraveled into soft, fragmented cries. Reever felt it begin for her, felt the tiny convulsions deep inside her. She opened her eyes and looked right into his, and her voice shattered as she called his name in surprise at the fire consuming her until she couldn't breathe, couldn't see, could do nothing but come apart in his arms. He held her tightly, rocking against her slowly, sweetly, deeply, holding back his own release with all his strength because he wanted it never to stop for her or for him. He wanted always to be deep inside her, to feel ecstasy ripple through her body, to hear his name a broken cry on her lips, to have it last until he died.

Then Reever could hear Tory's cries no longer because he was calling her name as the world unraveled in slow motion, control slipping away from him in a series of soft, fierce explosions that were like nothing he had ever known.

Hot. Deep. Forever.

Eight

The meadow was exquisite, unexpected. On a stage of green grass, wildflowers swayed like dancers in the wind. Dense, nearly black pines ringed the meadow on three sides. On the fourth, low granite cliffs rose in a ragged stairway winding along the brilliant blue of Wolf Lake. Wolf Creek swirled gracefully across the meadow, murmuring and flashing through sunlight and shadow alike. A small cedar lodge had been built just below the crest of a ridge overlooking the meadow. The lodge's windows shone with the same clear silver light as the creek.

A new road snaked over the ridge and on out to the county road two miles beyond. A faint trail led from the lodge to the lakeshore. Other meadow trails were being marked out by the ranch hands. The trails in the surrounding forest required more work. The sound of axes biting into wood rang through the silence, telling of men hard at work clearing paths for dudes who had never been on a horse, much less in a forest that hadn't changed since Indians once glided through the shadowed silence in search of game.

"Payton was right about one thing," Tory said. She glanced sideways at Reever, who was standing next to her as they let their horses rest. "This is a beautiful place just to be alive in."

Reever smiled and ran his fingertip down Tory's cheek to her lips. "Yes," he said.

Tory's heart stopped, then beat more quickly. In the past two weeks Reever had been so gentle and loving with her that sometimes it was all she could do not to cry. Never once had he been harsh or impatient with her, no matter what the provocation. It was as though he were trying to erase even the memory of seeing her eyes darken at his cutting words. He had taught her to ride and had nothing but praise for her grace and quickness while she learned. It was the same when he worked with her in the garden. He had been almost as excited as she was by the exuberant growth of the plants.

A pair of cowboy boots had turned up next to her chair at breakfast a week ago, just as the work gloves once had. All the men denied any knowledge of how the boots had gotten there. This time she believed the men. She had seen Reever's face as he eased her feet into the polished leather as though the boots were crystal slippers left over from a fabulous ball. This morning it had been a hat that had appeared without warning, a soft, cream-colored Stetson that fit her perfectly.

Tory had tried to tell Reever that she couldn't let him give her anything else after the boots. He had smiled and stroked her hair and told her that it must have been the tooth fairy because he had never seen the hat before in his life. Then he had brushed her lips lightly with his thumb, stilling her words and caressing her in a single warm touch. She hadn't been able to prevent the two tears that had spilled down her cheeks, tears that he had caught on the edge of his thumb and then brought to his lips.

She had almost told him then. The words had ached in her throat as she loved him silently because he would not allow her to say the words aloud. But they were true just the same. She loved him until it was an agony and an ecstasy radiating through her silence, through her soul.

"Don't look at me like that," said Reever, his voice husky.

"Like what?"

"Like the sun rises and sets in my eyes."

"But it does," Tory said simply. Before Reever could voice the objections darkening his eyes, she smiled and added lightly, "That's what happens when you face east early in the morning and west late in the day. Even a city girl knows that much, cowboy."

Reever hesitated, then smiled, shaking his head. "Some city girl you turned out to be. I can't believe it—dinner was late last night because you were out in the barn helping a heifer have her first calf. Lord, little one, I've seen men turn pale and run rather than help pull a calf. Not you. You lay right down next to me in the straw and pulled for all you were worth. By the time we got back in the house, you were wringing wet and covered with stuff from head to toe."

"I'd do it again in a minute," Tory said, her face softening as she remembered the big-eyed, incredibly long-lashed, wobbly little calf butting at its mother's belly in an instinctive search for milk. "To walk into a stall where there's only one cow and to walk out later and leave two cows behind—that's as close to a miracle as I've ever come." Her face changed as she focused on him again. "Except with you, Reever," she whispered. "When you make love to me, it's not just the sun rising and setting in your eyes, it's the whole world burning."

For a moment Reever was very still. He searched Tory's eyes as though trying to see right through to her soul. After a long silence he said, "It's like that for me. Every time is better than the last until I can hardly wait to wrap myself around you again and wrap you around me until—" He shuddered and his eyes darkened as the familiar wild heat began to sweep through him again. "Oh, God, little one. You're in me hotter and deeper than my own blood."

Abruptly Reever turned and mounted Blackjack. "I'd better see if Jed has managed to gnaw through that big pine yet," he said, reining around until he could look at Tory. "And I'd better do it now before I pull you down in the grass and love you until you cry and scream and come apart in my arms."

"Reever," Tory said shakily, her breath shortening. "I want that. No. I want *you* like—like—"

"Hell on fire," he finished, his voice almost harsh. "I know. It's the same way I've wanted you since the first time I saw you. Close your eyes, little cat."

"Why?" she asked, closing her eyes.

Reever bent over in the saddle, lifted Tory in his powerful arms and kissed her with a thoroughness that left both of them aching.

"Keep those beautiful green eyes closed," he said hoarsely. "It's the only way I'll be able to leave you."

Slowly Reever eased Tory back onto her feet, took one more quick, biting kiss and spun Blackjack around. Tory didn't open her eyes until the sound of the horse's hooves had faded. Then she let out a long, tremulous breath and mounted Twinkletoes. She guided the gentle mare along a path leading to the beach that the hands had cleared along the lake.

"Hi, Dutch. How's the fire ring doing?"

The wiry cowboy dropped a water-smoothed stone as big as a basketball into the ring he was building. "Slow, Tory. Real slow. Been trying to figure how to do it from the back of a horse."

Tory smiled. She had learned that all the hands wanted only the work that could be done from horseback. "Are you going to be here for a while?"

"Yep. Going swimming again?"

"Sure am."

Dutch shook his head. "How something as sweet as you don't melt in all that water is beyond me. Ain't natural."

"I think someone I know is angling for peach cobbler again," muttered Tory.

He smiled innocently. "Cobbler? You making cobbler tonight? Did I ever tell you that peach is my favorite?"

"Really?" she asked, feigning astonishment.

Dutch chuckled, winked and went back to sorting rocks for the fire ring. Tory tied Twinkletoes to a handy bush, pulled a rolled-up towel from her saddle bag and went toward a long tongue of granite that ran out into the lake. There she peeled down to the swimsuit she wore beneath her riding clothes.

Twelve days ago, when Reever had decided it was time to put the finishing touches on "Payton's Folly," Tory had discovered that one of the springs beneath Wolf Lake was hot. That, and the lure of clean, deep water, had been too great to ignore after months of abstinence. The first time Tory had gone swimming there had been a line of appreciative cowhands watching her. While Reever hadn't wanted her to swim alone, he didn't figure that she needed every man within fifty miles as a lifeguard. When he couldn't do the job himself, he had assigned Dutch to beach, fire ring and lifeguard duty because Reever knew that Dutch's interest in Tory was strictly avuncular.

The water along the cobbled shoreline was decidedly brisk. The hot spring's influence didn't reach that far, and it was too early in the season for the sun to have made much impression on the overall temperature of the lake. Only at the base of the lower cliff was the water warmed by the hidden spring far beneath the surface of the lake.

Tory entered the water in a long, running dive and then swam toward the cliffs fifty yards away. The color of the water beneath her changed as the bottom dropped steeply away. Close to the cliffs she had no idea how deep the water was. That was one of the things she was going to find out today.

With the ease of someone to whom water is a second home, Tory jackknifed her body and dove straight down. The pressure around her built swiftly. Automatically she swallowed, letting her ears adjust. All around her was clear, very blue water. There were no rocks, no dead trees, no obstacles of any kind. She continued down until she was sure that she was beyond thirty feet, then she flip turned and headed back for the shimmering silver surface.

Tory slung hair out of her face with a casual motion of her head, pulled up her swim goggles and saw that Dutch was watching intently. She waved, swam about twenty feet, pulled her goggles into place and dove again. Methodically she quartered the area beneath the lowest cliff, looking for any surprises that might be hidden by the water. She didn't expect to find any. Yesterday she had stood on the lower cliff and looked over the water very, very carefully, coming at different times of day to take advantage of different angles of sunlight penetrating the unusually clear water. She had seen nothing to suggest any danger to someone diving from the granite shelf that overhung the deep water.

Nor did Tory find anything dangerous as she physically inspected the area below the base of the cliff. The granite wall was smooth all the way down. It had a slight over-hang, ensuring that no matter how badly botched a dive might be, there was no way of landing on rock. The water beneath the overhang was deep, clean and as free of obstructions as a diving pool.

Tory swam back to shore, pulled on the beach walkers she had carried in her towel and picked her way along the shoreline as it gradually humped up into the first of a series of steplike cliffs. The way to the top of the lowest cliff that she had found was short and quite safe, for the path didn't come near the edge of the rock. She stepped out onto the smooth, nearly flat granite platform.

Shivering slightly in the breeze, Tory stood at the knife-edge of the cliff. To her right more granite rose steeply, notching the sky. To her left the granite merged gently with the beach. Below her the lake shimmered and rippled in shades of blue, whispering to her. She knew that the cliff was almost exactly ten meters high. She knew because all her senses had been attuned to that height by thousands and thousands of dives off ten-meter platforms. It felt... right... standing there, looking down into the lake.

The temptation to dive was almost overwhelming. Tory had been working her knee for at least an hour every night, often more. Time went quickly as she braced herself against Reever's powerful arm and exercised while he talked about the ranch and his tangled family history. She had told him about her own family and her years spent around the swim club's Olympic pools. And sometimes there was a sweet silence while he watched her with clear gray eyes, smiling gently, approving of her without saying a word.

Yet despite all the exercises, all the care that Tory had taken not to stress the knee again, she was afraid that it wasn't as strong as her left knee. There was no way for her to be sure without diving.

For a long time Tory stood on the cliff looking into the depths of Wolf Lake as though it held the answers to her questions about the future. Wind ruffled the water's surface, making ghostly silver patterns. Gradually Tory realized that she was shivering with something more than cold. She turned her back on the sapphire depths and hurried down the trail.

"You sure do like that cliff, don't you?" asked Dutch, looking up as Tory went by dressed in her riding clothes again. "You can see everything from there, can't you?"

"Almost," she said quickly, shivering, not wanting to talk.

Once back at the lodge, Tory went to her room and changed into dry clothes. One wing of three bedrooms and the kitchen were the only parts of the lodge and cottages that were completely finished. The rest waited for carpenters and painters who always seemed to be busy elsewhere. Not that Reever was complaining; he wouldn't care if the Sundance Retreat never opened. Tory halfway suspected that he was paying the workers not to show up.

Tory hurried into the kitchen and stopped, astonished to find that Reever was there, calmly browning meat for chili on the lodge's big gas stove.

"If you make the biscuits," he said, looking up, "we can have supper all ready to go. Then we can sneak away for a ride to that tiny hidden meadow I told you about."

Tory's sudden smile made Reever wonder if he had ever seen anything half so beautiful. He smiled in return, holding out his hand to her, bringing her fingers to his lips. He rubbed his mustache against her inner wrist and traced the lines of her veins with the tip of his tongue.

"Can you make biscuits one-handed?" he asked in a low voice, biting the pad of flesh at the base of her thumb.

Slowly she shook her head.

"Damn." Reluctantly Reever released Tory's hand. "Show me how fast you can make biscuits, little cat."

As soon as Tory's heartbeat settled down, it took her very little time at all to get the rest of the dinner ready. Hand in hand, she and Reever walked down to the corral, which was little more than a series of ropes strung between pine trees. Twinkletoes was there, but not Blackjack.

"I told Teague that he could use Blackjack," Reever said casually. "We'll double up on Twinkletoes. It's about time you learned how to ride bareback anyway." He grinned down at Tory. "Don't look so worried. Twinkletoes is so placid you could hang upside down from her belly and she'd never notice. And you can hang on to me as much as you want."

Reever buried his left hand in Twinkletoes's mane, took one step and vaulted onto the mare's back in a single flowing movement, making no more fuss about mounting than if he had used a stirrup.

"Close your mouth, city girl. You'll catch flies," teased Reever.

"How did you do that?" demanded Tory.

"Practice. Strength doesn't hurt, either."

"No kidding," she said dryly. "Any other suggestions?"

"Hold out your left arm. Grab my left arm just above the elbow," he said, leaning down to her. "Step onto my boot just like it was a stirrup."

Tory did and found herself being lifted through the air and swung into place behind Reever. The first thing she noticed was the sensation of warmth radiating up from Twinkletoes through her jeans. The second thing was the ripple and play of powerful muscles as the mare shifted her weight.

The third thing was the fact that, short of actually making love, there was no greater physical intimacy possible for a man and a woman than riding double, bareback.

"Ready?" asked Reever.

"What a question," Tory muttered.

He looked over his shoulder, saw her dilating pupils and knew just what was happening to her. The same thing was happening to him. He had been looking forward to this ride for a long time. He smiled slowly, wickedly.

"Wrap your arms around me," Reever said. When Tory did, he twisted in slow motion, rubbing his back sensually across her breasts, caressing her. He heard her breath come in suddenly as her back arched, increasing the sweet pressure of his touch. "Ah, little cat," he said huskily, "I can feel your nipples asking for me. I'm going to make you wait, though. I'm going to make you as wild as my dreams."

Tory's breath shivered out as Reever's big, hard hand traced the length of her thigh nestled so intimately against his. "I'll get even with you," she said in a trembling voice. "I swear it."

"God, honey, I hope so. Hang on."

A touch of Reever's heels sent Twinkletoes walking out into the sunlight that was slanting down between the erect, fragrant bodies of the pines. After the first few minutes Tory found it surprisingly easy to adjust to being bareback. If anything, the lack of a saddle helped her to find and move to the horse's rhythms more quickly. Before a mile had gone by, she relaxed completely against Reever and let the warmth of the sun, of the placid horse and of the man she loved seep into her.

Reever sensed Tory's adjustment to the new style of riding in the easy, rhythmic swaying of her body against his. Smiling, knowing that he could safely distract her now, he brought one of her hands up to his mouth. Gently he sucked on each finger in turn, biting lightly at the most sensitive flesh, softly devouring her until he heard her whimper deep in her throat. Then his teeth closed less gently on her palm until she shivered and arched against him, clinging to his hard warmth.

With aching sensuality Reever rubbed Tory's hands over his chest, turning and twisting against her like a cat until her nails found his tiny, hard male nipples and scraped sweetly over them. A groan wedged deep in his throat. He released her fingers, but she didn't stop caressing him. Her hands moved in the same sensual rhythms of the horse walking, and her body stroked his with each motion.

Tory pressed closer to Reever's powerful back even as her fingers slid between the snaps of his shirt. At the first hot touch of his flesh, she made a low sound. Slowly her hands tugged in opposite directions, unfastening the snaps on his shirt one by one. Her palms rubbed over him restlessly, hungrily, and her fingers dug softly beneath the thick hair. He moved against her touch, stroking her with his own body while fire pooled hotly, heavily between his thighs. He felt her hand search each ridge and swell of muscle on his chest even as her mouth pressed against his spine. Her teeth tugged at his shirt while her fingers flexed and buried themselves in the warm black thatch of hair curling over his chest.

Reever let go of the reins he had knotted together and pulled his shirt free of his jeans. Even before he had finished, he felt a hot rain of kisses across his naked back. Then, with a catlike sound of contentment, Tory caressed his skin with her cheek, turning her face from side to side as though he were a warm river and she were bathing in him. Her mouth opened and she shivered as she tasted him.

Reever's breath shortened. He felt as though he were caught between two fires, Tory's hands on his chest and her mouth caressing his back. His own hands began a slow, sweet stroking of her thighs until she rocked against him with more than the horse's easy motions. Slowly, inevitably, her hands slid down his chest to the less sensually rewarding material of his jeans. She stroked his hard thighs once and then again and again, using her fingernails and sliding higher up his legs each time until she finally brushed against the rigid proof of his desire.

"Tory—" grated Reever.

Her hands returned, settling over him sweetly, hotly.

"Let me," she breathed, closing her teeth on his back with the slow, loving sensuality he had taught her. "Help me."

Reever looked down and saw Tory's delicate fingers against the faded blue fabric as she stroked him. He knew he should stop her, but it was too much what he had dreamed of since the first day she had ridden behind him and he had ached at the thought of having her hands on him. When she tugged blindly at the fastening on his jeans, he shuddered heavily.

"Reever," Tory said, her hands trembling, her breath hot against his back. "Please."

Slowly he guided her fingers over his jeans until the cloth parted. Her hands eased inside his clothes. She made a husky sound of discovery and pleasure as she found him. Reever felt her touch like sweet fire over his aroused flesh. He stifled a groan as he shifted position, bringing himself more fully into her hands.

"I love touching you," Tory said huskily, and her breath flowed hotly over Reever's skin. "I love feeling you change and knowing you want me more and more with each heartbeat. Your whole body gets hard. Everywhere, not just where I'm holding you now." Her teeth closed over a muscle that rippled beneath the taut, naked skin of his back.

"You're so strong," she whispered. "I love your strength. I love the salty taste of your skin. I love your heat. I love—"

At the last instant Tory controlled the tumbling words, dragging herself back from the brink of admitting how much she loved Reever himself.

"Everything," she said finally, caressing him, measuring his potency, savoring the different textures that went from hot satin smoothness to the tight male flesh hidden within a thatch of hair. "I love everything about you, Reever."

"Oh, God," Reever groaned. The sight of Tory's slender fingers loving him was like being connected to an electric current. He shuddered convulsively, repeatedly, a man being softly, wildly devoured. "Stop," he said thickly. "You'll make me lose control."

"Then I'd just have to start all over again, wouldn't I?" Tory asked. She laughed softly and bit his back hard enough to leave a small mark. "I can hardly wait."

Reever endured it for a few moments longer, watching Tory's hands like sweet flames caressing him, burning him. And then he felt forerunners of the release to come shuddering through him. He called her name, trying to still her hands, but it was too much like his dream, sweet and wild, inevitable, and the knowledge that she was shaking almost as much as he was only made it hotter.

When he finally managed to ease her hands up his body and refastened his jeans, he kissed her palms lovingly and stroked her arms, trying to calm her. It was a long time before they both could breathe without air catching in their throats. Only then did Reever stop Twinkletoes, bring his right leg over her neck and slide off.

"Reever?" asked Tory.

"Scoot forward and lean to the right, little cat. It's your turn. And mine."

Tory didn't understand, but she did as Reever had asked. He swung up behind her in a single swift motion, reached around her and picked up the reins. A gentle nudge of his heels sent Twinkletoes ambling up the dim trail. He let go of the knotted reins, knowing that the mare would keep walking without his guidance.

"I was going to ride this way from the first," Reever said, pulling Tory even closer against his body, "but I didn't trust myself to get all the way to the meadow. Then I discovered that you're every bit as bad—and as good—as I am."

Tory gave Reever a puzzled look over her shoulder, still not understanding. He smiled down at her with such sensual promise that her lips parted on a sudden intake of breath. He caught her chin and licked her lips delicately, nibbling and tugging as though it were her breast rather than her mouth he was teasing. The promise implicit in his caress made Tory's nipples tingle and tighten in a rush that sent fire racing through her core.

"They know, don't they?" whispered Reever, biting the nape of Tory's neck as his hands settled around her ribs, pulling the T-shirt tight to reveal her hard nipples.

"What?" she asked.

"Your breasts," he said, rubbing his palms along her ribs. "See? They're changing for me." Just above the tight crowns his fingers traced circles that touched only air. Even so, she rose and tightened visibly, as though she had been stroked. "They know I'm going to love them with my hands and my mouth." His voice deepened as his fingers drifted down her body to her thighs. "Does the rest of you know that, honey? Are you changing for me where I can't see you?"

Tory shivered and Reever smiled.

"I'm going to find out," he said, tasting her neck as he caressed her thighs. "But not right away." His hands eased up to her ribs again, and this time he was beneath the soft cotton of her T-shirt. His touch skirted her breasts, defining them without touching them.

"Reever," she said huskily, turning toward him, trying to capture his elusive touch. "You're torturing me."

"No, I'm not," he said, laughing softly. "Not yet. But soon, little cat. Soon I'm going to hold your breasts in my hands. I'm going to stroke and tug on those pink buds until something flowers deep inside you. Then I'm going to undo your jeans and find another bud, another flowering, but this one won't be hidden inside you. This one I'll be able to tease and love until I have to hold you on Twinkletoes because you'll forget where you are, who you are, everything but my touch on your sweet, hungry body."

Tory tried to speak, could not and shivered instead. Reever smiled as he watched the march of sensation over his lover's smooth skin.

"I can't wait any longer," he said. His voice was very deep as his teeth caressed her neck with fierce restraint. "I've dreamed about this since I brought you back to the ranch on Blackjack weeks ago. But Blackjack isn't placid like Twinkletoes, and you couldn't ride worth a damn then. It's different now. Lift your arms for me, honey. Let me show you what a woman like you does to a man like me."

Slowly Tory lifted her arms over her head. Reever spread his big, warm fingers and eased the T-shirt up over her body without touching her skin. The sliding pressure of the cloth over her nipples made Tory's breath catch. Reever's left arm settled over her bare midriff while his right hand tucked her T-shirt safely inside the waistband of his jeans. He tightened his arm, bringing Tory fully against his body, giving him a view of the creamy curves and deep pink tips. His muscular forearm moved up to take the warm, soft weight of her breasts. The contrast between her pale, smooth skin and the tanned, black-haired power of his arm made Reever feel hot and very male.

"I feel like I've been waiting all my life to see you like this," Reever said, rubbing his forearm slowly against Tory. "All that long ride home I wanted to tear off that damned T-shirt and see those sweet buds against my skin. Then when my hand touched you like this—"

Tory's whole body stiffened as Reever's right hand skimmed over the aching peak of her breast.

"Yes," he said thickly. "You jerked just like that, like you'd been touched by a live wire. Is that how it feels when I touch you, honey? So good it almost hurts? It feels like that when you touch me."

"Reever," Tory moaned, seeing his hand so close to her but not giving her what she needed as much as she needed air. "Oh, Reever, please—"

"You get so hard," he said, his voice deep and dark. He shifted his hands until her breasts filled his palms and his fingers could capture the taut nipples. "I love seeing you, feeling you, knowing that I've done this to you. And then I love doing this." His fingers closed, tugging at her, rolling her between his sensitive fingertips until her hips began to move in the primal rhythms of passion.

"Tell me what it feels like," Reever said, his voice soft, hoarse.

"Wires—tightening," Tory said raggedly. "All through me. Hot—sweet—wires." She arched against his hands, silently asking for a harder touch.

"Put your hands over mine, honey. Show me how to make it feel even better for you. Don't be shy," he murmured when he saw the blush rising up her neck. He released her breasts, not touching her. "I want to know how to love you," he said huskily. "I want this to be your dream, too. Or didn't you want my hands on you all that long ride home? Didn't you ever dream about riding double with me, naked, and having me love you until you came apart? I dreamed about it, little cat. And every time I dreamed, I woke up shaking, sweating, wild."

Breath shuddered through Tory. The sunlight and air caressed her breasts, but that wasn't enough. She looked down and saw Reever's hard, tanned fingers on her thighs and saw the aching, rose-tipped hunger of her breasts. Slowly she pulled his hands up her body until they enveloped her. She turned from side to side, dragging her sensitive peaks across his palms, holding him close, hard. When his fingers caught her nipples, she shuddered and moaned her approval as she rubbed her cheek against his chest, needing the masculine textures of hair and hard muscle.

Reever watched Tory's eyes close while sensations shivered through her, making her whole body taut. He continued the sweet torment of her breasts until her cheeks were flushed and her breath came quickly, hotly. Then he tilted her face up to his and kissed her while his hand caressed the length of her body once and then again. The third time his hand moved over her jeans, they came undone. Long, lean fingers slid inside the tiny triangle of Tory's briefs.

The ragged cry Tory gave when Reever rhythmically stroked her was a sound from his dreams. His hands closed sweetly, fiercely, on her breast and between her thighs, holding her in a sensual vise while his teeth caressed the nape of her neck. Her hips lifted instinctively into his touch, giving more of herself to him. With a thick sound of satisfaction, he took her silky secrets while his thumb teased the hard bud concealed within her softness. She began to twist slowly, consumed by his touch. He whispered to her, asking her what she wanted, giving it to her even as she answered, feeling her melt and run like wild honey beneath the hot skill of his hands.

"Reever—" Tory's voice broke as his thumb moved slowly, smoothly, making her shiver, pleasure showering through her with each touch. "No more," she cried finally. "I can't—I'm going to—"

"Then I'll just have to start over again, won't I?" Reever said, repeating what she had told him a few minutes before. He smiled down at her, his eyes a silver blaze of passion and anticipation. "Only with you, little cat, it isn't a case of starting over like it is for me. The second time you'll start higher, and then I'll take you even higher, all the way to the other side of the sun."

Tory tried to speak but could not. Her body was no longer hers. Reever had stolen it one caress at a time until she could only twist in slow motion against him, covering his fingers with her own, teaching and learning at the same time until she gave a husky cry and arched like a drawn bow in his hands. He cradled her against his hot body, holding her in place on the horse's broad back. Slowly he kissed her flushed cheek and caressed her very gently, bringing her back to herself. When she gave a long, trembling sigh, he smiled and touched her hot skin with his open mouth.

"That's just the beginning," Reever murmured, tasting the warm mist that passion had brought to Tory's skin. "Look around you. We've reached the meadow."

Tory's eyes opened slowly. All around her grass grew thickly, and the air was heavy with the scent of flowers unraveled by the sun. Reever dismounted and lifted Tory from the mare's back into his own arms. He walked to a small rise and sank to his knees in the cool grass. Tory's eyes darkened until they were the intense summer green of the grass as she watched her lover bending down to her, his expression intent, dark, heavy with sensuality. Slowly he undressed her and then himself. Very gently he parted her legs, caressing their smooth length, watching her with eyes the color of tarnished silver, eyes that promised . . . everything.

"I'm going to make love to you the way I've dreamed of it," Reever said in a husky, caressing voice as his fingertips traced the curves of Tory's legs. "You couldn't have accepted it before now. And neither could I before I met you. This will be a first for me, too."

Tory watched Reever with eyes that were almost frightened. He was more aroused than she had ever seen him. The sight of his naked need was a live wire brushing her, sweetly shocking every nerve to life, promising a passion that she had never known. As he knelt between her legs, she began to shiver under the impact of the primal sensuality radiating from him. He lowered himself over her, stroking all of her with a single slow movement of his powerful body.

Reever's open mouth moved over Tory's face, tasting her, feeling her, caressing her, knowing her with teeth and tongue and lips. She caught and held him with her mouth for a long, sweet moment, and his tongue promised her things she had never dreamed of. When he tore his mouth from hers, she whimpered softly. His mouth closed on her neck in a fierce caress that left a loving mark and drew a sound of surprise and passion from her lips. He laved the mark with his tongue before his mouth moved lower. He found a breast and consumed it as slowly and completely as he had consumed her mouth. It was the same for her other breast, tugged and suckled to a hard peak while she shivered and twisted beneath the loving demands of his tongue.

Reever's open mouth traced the line of Tory's ribs as he eased further down her body. She felt the sudden, hard warmth of his rigid tongue flicking into her navel again and again, sending surprising bursts of heat through her with each touch. When she slid her fingers into his hair to hold him closer, he bit her shivering flesh gently and slid further down her flushed body. As she had done when she drank from the creek, he rubbed his face against her body repeatedly, turning from side to side, caressing the tangled triangle of dark gold hair until she moaned. His hands stroked her inner thighs with subtle demand. Instinctively she yielded, opening to him even more. And then her whole body tightened at the first intimate touch of his mouth.

"It's all right," Reever said gently, biting Tory with exquisite delicacy. "You're almost ready now."

"For what?" she whispered, and her voice, like her body, trembled.

"To die with me inside you, and then to be born again the same way. With me. We're going to be together all the way to our souls."

Tory didn't answer. She couldn't. Sensations she had never known were sweeping through her, dragging fire in their wake. She called Reever's name and was answered by a caress that made her cry out at the incandescent pleasure bursting through her. The world slid farther away from her with each wave of fire, each consuming caress, until she could neither think nor speak, only respond with an abandon that was like nothing she had ever experienced.

With a final, slow caress Reever moved over Tory, wrapping himself around her, catching her wild cries with his mouth at the same instant that he thrust into her, burying himself in the sweet heat and ecstatic fire he had created. He felt the fierce, delicate, overwhelming completion take her even as he did. He moved slowly, fully, increasing and savoring her release as though it were his own. When the last shivering tremors finally faded from her softness, he held himself perfectly still, waiting for her eyes to open.

"Tory," he murmured, biting her lower lip with exquisite sensuality.

Her eyes opened and she stared straight into the hot silver of barely leashed, soul-deep desire. "Reever?"

"Yes, little cat," he said huskily. "Now it begins."

The first powerful movement of Reever's body made Tory gasp. The second movement inflamed nerves still shivering in the aftermath of ecstasy. The pleasure was so intense that she had to bite her lip against a scream. Desire burst through her as she felt every muscle in Reever's body become rigid with sensual tension. She smelled the heady, musky heat of his skin and was deeply aware of every motion he made within her. He moved again and then again, harder, deeper, faster, ripping the world away from her with each potent motion of his body.

Tory didn't know that her nails raked down Reever's back as she wept and shuddered and cried her wild ecstasy. She knew only that she could feel no greater pleasure without dying. She tried to tell Reever that she could bear no more, but no words came to her in her need, only explosions of greater and greater ecstasy. She couldn't breathe, couldn't move. Dimly she heard her name torn from his throat in a harsh, broken cry as his control burst into a shattering release. With all his power he locked himself so deeply within her that each pulse of his pleasure was a live current touching her. Her whole body shook with the violence of the ecstasy sleeting through her. Wave after wave of pleasure transformed her, wringing sweet cries from her as each expanding ring of ecstasy swept through her and burst.

Slowly, slowly, the world condensed again around Tory. There was the untamed blue of sky and the rippling green of summer grass and the tan of Reever's face as he watched Tory darkly. He was holding her with bruising strength, still locked deeply within her. Somewhere a voice whispered, *I love you, I love you, I love you,* as though a breath could not be taken without that elemental truth being spoken.

At first Tory thought that she was dreaming—and then she realized that she was awake, that Reever was watching her with eyes that were the color of steel and that it was her own voice whispering the forbidden words to him.

I love you.

Nine

For the hundredth time Tory relived the long, silent ride back to the ranch. Reever had been achingly tender with her, treating her as though she were made of the most fragile china. He had said nothing, done nothing to indicate that he had heard her helpless admission of love. But he had heard. She was sure of it.

He hadn't touched her since then.

Five days. Each day longer than the one before, shorter than the one to follow. It wasn't a return to the harshness of the time before they had become lovers. Reever continued to treat Tory with a gentleness that made her throat close around silent screams—because beneath that unfailing kindness she sensed him sliding away from her, retreating, easing apart from her so very carefully, not wanting to cause her any more pain.

He did not love her.

With each breath Tory took, that terrible certainty turned in her soul like a razor. She didn't even know if Reever desired her physically any more. He was so kind to her. Too kind. When he looked at her—if he looked at her at all—there was none of the leashed passion that once had turned his eyes to a smoky crystal blaze. There was only the kind of sorrow that made the razor of loss turn more deeply in her, her life bleeding away secretly, tears wept in darkness, unseen, unheard, untouched, unknown.

"Hi, Tory," said Dutch, shutting the lodge's kitchen door behind him and looking hopefully toward the huge, shining stove. "What's cooking?"

Tory blinked and looked down at her hands. She was cutting beef into cubes. That meant stew. Had she made stew last night or the night before? She couldn't remember. She hadn't even known what she was cooking until she looked down and saw the red chunks waiting to go into the seasoned flour.

"It looks like stew from here," she said.

"Great!" Dutch said enthusiastically. "We haven't had that for a week. Lots of gravy, okay?"

"Swimming in it," Tory promised, feeling as though she should make a note in the spilled flour on the counter before she forgot. She was living on automatic pilot. It had to stop. She had never been like this before, no matter how crushing a loss had seemed to her at the time.

Why won't Reever even talk to me? Why does he slide like water through my fingers every time I try to speak to him alone?

It would be different tonight. If there were no other way, she would wait until he went to bed, and then she would corner him in his bedroom. She would— "Watch it!" cautioned Dutch.

Even as he spoke, the knife that Tory was using slipped, drawing a red line over her finger. Without making a sound, she put down the knife, turned and went to the sink. She held her finger under the cold water streaming out of the faucet.

"Is it bad?" Dutch asked anxiously, hovering over her.

"Is what bad?" asked Reever from the doorway.

Tory's heart turned over just at the sound of Reever's voice. Her breath stopped, then came in harshly.

"She cut her finger," Dutch said.

"Let me see."

Tory shook her head, keeping her back turned to Reever, feeling hot and cold and dizzy, and her body shivered like a crystal glass struck by a careless hand. She was afraid. If Reever touched her, she would fall apart. She loved him. He had wanted her with a passion that had set them both afire. But now he didn't want her. She had waited, hoping with each hour, each minute, each second, that he would come to her. He had not. The longer she stayed close to him, the more unbearable her loss became. She was tearing herself apart, teetering on the instant of shattering.

The wild seething of Tory's emotions shocked her. In that moment she knew that she wouldn't corner Reever tonight or any other night. There was no reason to, except to hurt herself even more by refusing to accept the reality of her relationship with him. Reever had nothing to say to her that he hadn't already said—she had all the qualifications to be his lover and none of the ones to be his beloved. He had told her so the first day. She just hadn't believed him then.

She didn't want to believe him now. How could she love so deeply and not have it returned, even a little?

Dizzy, feeling the world slipping away from her grasp, Tory fought for self-control.

"Dutch, check on Blackjack, will you?" Reever said carefully, seeing the color drain completely from Tory's face. "I think his right foreleg might be swollen."

Dutch had just seen Blackjack, and the horse had never looked better. A glance at Reever's bleak eyes froze Dutch's protest in his throat. He turned and went out the back door without a word.

"Let me see it."

Reever's tone was gentle, coaxing, restrained . . . and somehow as distant as the moon.

"There's no need," Tory said, her voice thin. "It's just a scratch."

He didn't bother to argue. He simply took her hand from the stream of water and watched crimson blood well instantly from the cut. He also watched her helpless response to his touch, the shiver she couldn't control, and he heard the soft sound of her breath breaking. His eyes closed.

"Tory," Reever said achingly. "I didn't want it to be like this."

"Like what?" she asked faintly.

"You loving me."

"And you not loving me." Tory's eyes darkened as she looked out the kitchen window at the supple pines and the lake shimmering beneath the sun. "I believe you," she whispered. "I'll buy that bus ticket out of here, the one you've been telling me to get since the first time you saw me. You're free, Reever. Go find the perfect woman of your dreams. I'll go find the perfect platform, the perfect pool, the perfect dive, and then I'll step off into the air and float forever. . . ." As the last word died away, she shivered violently. "But thank you," she added, her voice thinned almost to breaking. "You made it so very good for me. When you held me, it was more beautiful than anything I'd ever dreamed."

Tory pulled her trembling hand from Reever's grasp, ignoring the line of scarlet sliding down her finger. The cut was only superficial. The rest of her wounding was not.

"I should have driven you into town that first day," Reever said, his voice suddenly as harsh as though he had never held her, never felt her come apart in his arms. His eyes were dark, nearly wild, savage. "I didn't want your virginity. I didn't want the guilt of taking a young girl without words of love. But you burned like a fire in me all the way to my soul. So I seduced a city girl who was only marking time until she could go back to the bright lights. That's what you were doing at the Sundance, isn't it, city girl? Marking time until your knee healed, until you could make that perfect dive. God, I wish I'd never touched you!"

The little color that had been left in Tory's world faded away. "My fault, Reever," she said, her voice so frail that it was almost like silence. "I can't say you didn't warn me. I know that I'm a long way from the woman of your dreams. You told me often enough. I just didn't listen very well, did I?"

In the sudden, taut silence the sound of cowboy boots stamping off mud on the flagstone walkway beyond the kitchen was as loud as an exchange of gunshots. Jed's voice rose over the noise, as did Miller's. Both of them were speculating on whether any of Tory's cookies were available for starving cowhands.

"Tell them the cookies are in the blue jar," Tory said, her voice breaking as she slipped past Reever.

When Tory finally came back to the kitchen, the room was empty of cookies, cowhands and Reever. The remaining meat was cubed and neatly stacked to one side of the cutting board. She didn't have to be told that Reever had taken care of it for her. With trembling hands she dredged the big cubes in the seasoned flour, browned them and set them aside to simmer slowly while she made four cherry pies.

Tory tried not to think, not to feel, but it was impossible. By the time dinner was ready, it was all she could do to force herself to sit at the table with Reever only inches away.

God, I wish I'd never touched you!

But he had. Nothing could change that. All that remained was for Tory to find a way to survive loving a man who didn't love her in return, not even a little.

"Tory, are you on some kind of damn fool diet?" asked Dutch.

"What?" she asked, startled out of her thoughts.

"You're not eating enough to keep a kitten alive," Dutch said gruffly. "You haven't for five days. I just wondered if you was on some damn fool diet. None of my business, of course, but you sure don't need to get any skinnier."

Tory looked down at the stew she had been pushing from one side of her plate to the other, and at the biscuit she had shredded without eating. It had been the same for every meal since Reever had taken her to the small meadow and made love to her until the truth poured out of her in husky, heedless cries.

"I—I ate too many cookies earlier," lied Tory. "Ruined my appetite."

Dutch gave her a skeptical look but said nothing more.

"I checked on your garden today," Jed said, reaching for another biscuit. "The drip that Reever set up in the furrows is keeping everything green, but I think the beans need some more of that fancy fertilizer. Want me to pick up a bag when I go into town for supplies tomorrow?"

"That would be very—" Tory cleared her throat. "Could I go in with you?" she asked urgently. "I have to—do something."

For an instant Jed looked surprised, then he grinned. "Sure thing, Tory. Too bad I'm not twenty-one yet. I'd buy you your first legal drink."

Tory sensed Reever's sudden, intent scrutiny. "What?" she asked.

"Don't you turn twenty-one tomorrow?" continued Jed, oblivious to Reever's narrowed, icy eyes. "Or is that next month?"

"Is tomorrow the thirtieth?" Tory asked.

"As ever was," Jed said, heaping butter on the biscuit.

"Oh," she said, swallowing. "Yes. My birthday."

"Wear your best jeans," said Jed. "I'll spring for lunch." He winked at the other men. "You see, I've got this thing for older women."

Reever's fork rang heavily against his dinner plate. Tory carefully did not look at him. She looked only at the steaming, fragrant, beautifully prepared and utterly unappealing dinner that she was systematically rearranging on her plate. Around her the hands argued about the best way to celebrate her birthday. She ignored them because it would have been too painful to speak, to tell them that their argument was academic. Whenever they celebrated her birthday, the guest of honor would be absent.

"But don't worry, boys," Jed continued blithely, "I'll get Tory back in time to cook dinner, birthday or no birthday. Otherwise, you'd all skin me alive."

This time it was Tory's fork that rang loudly against her plate. She wasn't going to come back. She couldn't bear being on the Sundance any longer, so close to the man she loved, yet so very far away from being loved in return. With a brilliant, false smile she stood up.

"There's some pie in the oven," she announced, withdrawing quickly from the dining area.

"Tory?" called Dutch.

She answered without looking back. "Just leave the dishes on the table. I'll take care of them when I've finished my knee exercises."

Reever's chair scraped loudly against the unglazed tile floor as he pushed back with a force just short of violence.

"Boss?" asked Jed, looking surprised.

"I'm going to check on Blackjack," snarled Reever.

Dutch, who knew that there wasn't anything wrong with Reever's favorite horse, wisely kept his mouth shut.

Tory went to her room and did her exercises, trying very hard not to think of Reever as she braced herself awkwardly on the wall, bumping her knee or her foot with every motion. The knee, at least, seemed better. It was neither tender nor swollen, and it had been a long time since she had limped at all. In that way, if in no other, the Sundance had been just what the doctor had ordered.

As soon as the exercises were finished, Tory pulled out her duffel bag and began cramming clothes into it, wondering why she felt so lost. For the first time in months she knew exactly where she was going—back to Southern California and the swim club, back to the diving that she loved and the competition that she had come to realize she didn't like at all. But competition was part of the only world that remained to her. Diving.

Going back. Going home. Going away from the man she loved, the man who did not love her.

Halfway through the packing, Tory found herself standing motionless, staring out the window as the moon rose, full and round and silver, brilliant with promises that would never be kept.

Don't be ridiculous, she told herself. *It's the same moon that you'll see tomorrow and tomorrow and tomorrow. Same world. Same everything. Except Reever and the*

Sundance. They'll be gone. Tomorrow and tomorrow and tomorrow.

Abruptly Tory turned away from the window. She realized that the lodge was utterly quiet. Making no noise, she walked out into the lodge's main room, which gave her a view of the dining area. The men had long since finished dinner and gone to the half-finished cottages where they slept. Reever was nowhere in sight.

Quickly Tory cleaned up the kitchen and returned to her room. She knew that she didn't need to hurry for fear of running into Reever. He would be with the men as he had been for the past five nights, playing poker and swapping lies until he thought she was asleep. Only then would he come quietly into the lodge, walking in his stockinged feet past her door, taking the bedroom at the end of the hall, as far away from her as he could get without causing a stir by sleeping out with the hands.

But Tory was never asleep when Reever came walking softly past her door. She was lying awake, afraid to breathe, praying with every bit of her strength that he would open the door and come to her, whispering words of love. It hadn't happened. It wouldn't happen tonight, either. He didn't love her. He didn't even want her anymore. Hanging around the ranch and hoping that he would change his mind was destroying her, and she knew it.

You've lost him, she told herself fiercely. *Accept it like you've accepted other losses. Accept it and get on with your life.*

It was late when Tory finished the last of her packing and crawled into bed. Suddenly, she knew that she couldn't go through it again. She couldn't lie awake until she heard Reever climb the lodge's front steps. She couldn't wait with her breath held and her body trembling while he ghosted toward her room. She couldn't bear to know again the terrible emptiness that came when he passed by her door as though she had never been born.

Nor could Tory tolerate being inside her room a moment longer. She threw aside the sheet and walked barefoot through the lodge. The screen door squeaked loudly in the absolute silence of the night, startling her for a moment before she shut the door and left the lodge behind. The path to the lake was a pale ribbon unwinding beneath a moon whose brilliance pressed sharp shadows from the trees. The air was warm, silky, so clear that the night was like an immense, transparent black bell whose ringing was expressed in the shattered brilliance of stars.

The cliffs rose in tones of gleaming pewter at the margin of the lake. Tory climbed the familiar trail easily, quickly, for she had come there many times and sat on the lowest cliff, looking down into the lake's thousand shades of blue. Tonight there was no breeze to disturb the pristine mystery of the lake's surface. It was like the night itself, deep, motionless, unknowable. It lay at her feet in a black-and-silver stillness that was uncanny. The moon's trail on the water was utterly sharp and so brilliant that it was painful to look upon for more than an instant.

Tory sat at the edge of the cliff's granite platform and looked down into the darkness and moonlight pooled beneath her feet. Shapes seemed to condense on the lake's surface as though on a shimmering black screen, shadows thrown by her mind as she thought about her life on the eve of her twenty-first birthday. Her years had been shaped by her yearnings to make a place for herself in the world, but to do that, it had been necessary to please men who couldn't be pleased. First her father, then her stepfather, then a succession of coaches. And finally Ethan Reever.

Ultimately she had failed in all cases, especially and most painfully with Reever.

Now she was going to buy a ticket back to a world that she no longer wanted, a world that might ruin her knee beyond recovery. Although she had exercised faithfully, sometimes painfully, every night in her room, the feeling had slowly grown in her that her right knee would never again be as strong as her left. Under most circumstances the difference wouldn't have been noticeable. Under the relentless stresses of world-class competition, it might be the margin between success and a crippling failure.

Narrow. Unnatural. Short-lived. Olympics. Get out and look at the world.

Fragments of the doctor's unwanted advice seemed to condense out of the night around Tory. She shivered and wrapped her arms around her knees, but it was her thoughts that chilled her, not the mild midnight air. The swim club had become home to her because she had no other and because she loved diving more than she had ever loved anything in her life.

Until Ethan Reever.

And the land. She had discovered that she loved the land, too, a love that had been eclipsed by her unexpected passion for a man. She loved being able to walk out into the night and to hear nothing but the sound of her own footsteps, her own breath, her own heartbeat. She loved standing on earth that had known the weight of millions of seasons and very few men. From the instant she had stepped down off the bus and seen distant, indigo mountains rising above a fertile land, something in her had uncurled from a tiny, hard seed and had begun to put down deep roots in the earth. Even now she could sense herself reaching toward the mountains, unfolding, growing, absorbing the beauty and the silence and the fragrant air.

She had been born in the city, but she had been born for the land.

With that certainty something eased inside Tory, dimming some of the pain that had paralyzed her. When she left in the morning, it wouldn't be to go back to the narrow world she no longer wanted. She would go to find a new world full of mountains and silence and tender grass swaying in the wind. There would be a place for her in that world—cook or waitress, cashier or baby-sitter, it didn't matter. There would be a way for her to eat and sleep and wake up surrounded by mountains and seasons. Part of her, at least, would finally have come home. As for the rest, it would either heal or she would adjust to living with pain. That, too, she had learned in the past.

But tonight, for a short time, for the last time, she would know again the beauty of being a leaf turning on a silver wind.

"This just isn't your night, boss," offered Dutch, raking in a modest mound of chips. "Never knew you to try to fill an inside straight like that."

Reever grimaced. He hadn't meant to do anything so stupid, but since he had heard the lodge's screen door squeak open and shut, he hadn't been able to keep even part of his mind on the cards. He kept wondering what Tory was doing out in the night, if she were crying or simply walking, if the light had come back into her eyes or if she still looked far too old to be so young.

Twenty-one. How young is that? he asked himself harshly. *A hell of a lot older than it ought to be. Being seduced and dumped does that to a girl. What did she ever do to you but be the kind of lover you've always wanted and never had? For this crime you refuse to touch her? For this crime you're tearing her apart?*

And me, he thought bleakly. *I never knew how much it could hurt just to be alive. But then I never knew how much I could want a woman. City girl. Soft and sweet and just passing through the countryside. Too young to know what she really wants. Too young to know what love really is.*

But I know. It's like the land—enduring. It's a fire in the soul as well as the body. I know that, but she's too young to know it, no matter what soft words she says when she comes apart in my arms.

I wish to Christ I'd never touched you, city girl. Letting go of you is tearing me apart.

With a soft, vicious curse that made the cowhands look at each other uneasily, Reever picked up the cards he had been dealt. Faces stared back at him, faces laughing, crying, transformed by passion, pale with the kind of pain that he had never wanted her to feel. Tory's face repeated endlessly, her voice calling his name in all the shades of longing and love as she gave herself to him without reservation.

Too damned young!

Reever realized that the men were utterly silent, watching him. He saw the cards crushed within his fist. As he slowly opened his fingers, mutilated cards fell to the tabletop. Without a word he got up and walked out into the night.

Tory wasn't in the stable. She wasn't feeding carrots to Twinkletoes or leaning over the stall door talking to Blackjack. She wasn't standing in the small meadow behind the lodge. She wasn't anywhere in sight.

Without breaking stride, Reever took one of the three paths down to the lake. He carried no flashlight because he needed none. In the full moonlight it was bright enough to read print. The path went through a stand of pines and from there down the gentle slope to the lake. At one point, just before the descent to the shore, another trail snaked off toward the low granite cliffs. Reever didn't even look that way. He expected to find Tory along the moon-washed beach, watching tiny wavelets come apart.

There was no one along the shore. Reever felt a disappointment that was just short of pain. He searched the rocky beach again, unable to believe that Tory wasn't there. He had been so sure he would find her. He walked the shore with long strides, wondering if she might be hidden in the shadow of the cliffs.

As he reached the middle of the beach, a pale flash of movement caught Reever's eye. He looked up to his right, where a low granite cliff glowed like pewter in the moonlight. When he realized what he was seeing, he froze in disbelief.

Tory had been sitting so quietly that he had overlooked her. Then she had stood and thrown off her nightshirt. As naked as the moonlight itself, she walked with measured steps away from the edge of the cliff, turned as gracefully as a dancer and walked back toward the brink. With each step she moved faster, gathering herself, her intention clear in the elegant, poised tension of her body.

No! Stop!

The desperate cry went no farther than Reever's mind. It was too late. Tory had reached the brink and sprung up and outward. Arms spread wide, body perfectly arched, she floated on the air as though she were truly the swan from which her dive had taken its name. At the last possible instant her arms came together over her head, her body straightened and arrowed downward. She entered the midnight lake in a dive so perfectly executed that the water was barely disturbed.

The breath came out of Reever in a harsh rush when he saw Tory surface and swim cleanly toward the beach. Distantly he realized that he was trembling. When she rose naked from the lake and walked up the long tongue of granite leading to the shore, she didn't see him, for her eyes were turned back toward the cliff. Without hesitating, she climbed the trail to the top again.

Reever could have called out, could have stopped Tory, but he was frozen in the moment when she had dived into the lake with a grace and beauty that had literally taken his breath. He had not known that such a dive was possible.

Again Tory walked to the edge of the cliff, turned, paced a few steps away, then turned again, long legs eating up the distance to the brink. Her legs flexed and she arched up and out again. Her body bent at the hips, and she fell, turning and gleaming in the moonlight, describing a whole, incredibly slow circle that ended just in time for her to arrow cleanly into the water once more. Instants later she surfaced and swam for the ghostly tongue of granite.

Reever watched Tory leave the lake and climb the cliff trail again. She was like a condensation of moonlight, silent, shimmering with liquid silver, her feminine curves and hollows caressed by velvet touches of night. If he hadn't seen the dark, wet marks of her passage over the granite tongue, he would have thought he was dreaming.

Again the steps, the turn, the gathering speed, the leap into darkness. This time her arms came against her body at shoulder and hip, and she spun quickly, a gleaming whirlwind that became a woman only at the last possible instant, parting black waters with clean silence. Soon she was on the cliff again, leaping, soaring, spinning, falling, and then again and yet again, each dive more complex, more difficult, more beautiful than the one before.

Reever watched without moving, transfixed by Tory's skill. He had never known that the human body could be so elegant—and so ruthlessly disciplined in the search for perfection. He had never even imagined that such perfection was possible. Yet even as he silently celebrated Tory's extraordinary grace, he felt part of himself sliding down into a grim blackness that knew no end.

He had been wrong. No matter what her years were or were not, Victoria Wells was not a young girl. Not in any way that counted. She knew what was real and what was not, what was enduring and what was transient. That knowledge was shouted from every elegant movement, every difficult dive. He was watching the culmination of years of enormous discipline and effort. Few adults were capable of that kind of sustained sacrifice for a distant goal. Tory had been, even as a child. The truth of it was written in every beautiful line of her body turning and falling so perfectly through the night.

Another truth was written, too. As Reever stood and watched helplessly, he realized that he had come out tonight to find Tory, to hold her, to make love to her until pain was no longer possible.

Instead, he had lost her, and pain was all that was possible.

You never had her, cowboy, Reever told himself bleakly. *Look at her. You've never seen her equal. No one has. You might have made her sweet body sing, but you never could have competed with a lifetime of work and dreams. You finally found your woman—and it's too damned late. She has another life, other dreams. She's earned every one of them, too. All you can do is say goodbye.*

Reever lost count of the dives and the passage of time. He stood motionless, caught in a terrible net of beauty and despair until Tory stumbled slightly as she came out of the water, breaking Reever's bittersweet enchantment. He walked out of the shadows and lifted her into his arms. Her skin was wet, cool, as pale as moonlight. She was shivering. He held her and looked down at her face and knew that he had lost more than he could name.

"I just—" Tory's voice fragmented when she looked up into Reever's empty, tarnished eyes. "I just wanted to say goodbye," she whispered, almost frightened by the silence and the bleak emotions she sensed beneath his dark surface.

Reever's only answer was to hold Tory closer as he turned and walked back to the lodge, carrying her as though she weighed no more than his own shadow. Tory watched him silently, feeling caught within a dream. The sadness etched into Reever's expression made tears run like moonlight down her face. Only the warmth of his big body seeping into hers, driving away the lake's midnight chill, made her believe that the moment was real, that she wouldn't awaken and find herself alone, crying for him.

Without a word Reever carried Tory through the lodge to his own room. Moonlight poured in a silver torrent through the windows, transforming everything it touched. Tory trembled as she felt herself lowered to the bed.

"R-Reever?"

His mouth brushed darkly, warmly, over hers.

"Let me say goodbye, too," he said simply.

The words sliced into Tory like black crystal knives, but she did not cry out her protest. She loved Reever too much to turn away from him, from her impossible dream. Silently she watched him undress, loving him with every breath, every look. When he came down onto the bed beside her and gathered her against his warm body, tears welled from her eyes at the beauty of being held by him again.

Reever buried his face against Tory's neck and his arms locked powerfully, immovably around her, as though he would absorb her through his skin into his bones. Tremors went through him. As she felt the searing heat of tears sliding down her skin, Tory knew that it wasn't desire that was shaking Reever's powerful body. With a soundless cry she held him, sharing his pain without understanding its source.

After a long, long time Reever's grip loosened. He kissed Tory's eyelids softly, closing them, knowing that if he saw her watching him he would forget the promises he had made to himself and beg her to stay with him. He couldn't live with himself if he did that. She deserved the life she had trained so long to have.

Reever brushed his lips over Tory's, then dipped his tongue into her mouth for a single instant. The taste of her swept through him violently, almost overwhelming him. He wondered then how he had lived for five days without her . . . and how he would live for the rest of his days, days without number or end, a hell of his own making.

"When you told me you were leaving," Reever said, kissing the elegant line of Tory's neck and shoulder, her slanting cheekbone and soft lips, "I thought you had just used me to pass the time while your knee healed, and now you couldn't wait to get back." His mouth stilled the words he sensed forming on her lips. "No, little cat. Let me explain why I was so angry tonight. I don't want you to leave remembering only my devil temper."

Reever's mouth parted Tory's lips for the intimate caress of his tongue. He moved within her warmth slowly, loving and absorbing her until he felt her soften against him. Her tongue slid hotly over his, seeking to claim him in return. It was gentle agony to end the kiss, to withdraw his mouth by tiny increments until only the tip of his tongue could touch her.

"I didn't understand," Reever said huskily, kissing the smooth swell of Tory's breast. "I didn't realize what an incredibly good diver you are, what you must have given up to develop your skill and how passionately you must have wanted to be an Olympic diver to have achieved so much in so few years." He shuddered as his mouth tenderly traced the taut peak he had called out of her softness. "I didn't realize how beautiful the human body could be, either. You taught me that tonight. The memory of your diving will haunt me until I die. So elegant. So perfect." His voice dropped to a whisper. "You tore out my heart. That was when I knew what I had lost. You. My heart."

Tory's instinctive cry of protest was lost as Reever's hand gently covered her lips.

"Hush, little one," Reever said, trying to control the aching tumble of his words. "It's not your fault. You gave me only beauty, and I gave you—" His voice broke. For long moments there was only the soft, almost secret sound of Reever's hand smoothing over Tory's body. "It doesn't matter now," he said finally, his voice controlled again. "I just wanted you to know that I understand why you're leaving. There's nothing on the Sundance that can compare to what you've achieved. Nothing here can compete with your future as a diver. Not one thing. Certainly not the love of a man like me."

Tory shivered convulsively. She turned her face suddenly, eluding the hand that held her silent. "Reever—oh, God!" Her breath came in sharply. She was afraid even to hope. "Do you really care for me?" she whispered.

Reever's hands clenched on Tory's sweet body before he controlled himself. "You deserve more from life than I can give you. You've earned it, and then some. I'm going to see that you get it if I have to tie you on the bus myself. Otherwise, someday you'd hate me. You'd look at me and you'd see the man who stole your dream and called what he was doing 'love.' I couldn't take that, little cat. Anything, even losing you, but not stealing your dream the same way I stole your innocence."

Tory stared at the bleakness of Reever's eyes and knew that he meant every word.

"Do you know what I was saying goodbye to tonight?" she asked softly.

"To the summer," he said, turning his head from side to side against the softness of her breasts, caressing her as he spoke. "You were saying goodbye to your innocence, to the Sundance. To me."

"No!" Tory caught Reever's face between her hands and tilted it up to her, willed him to listen, to believe. "I was saying goodbye to diving, Reever, not to you!"

A shudder passed over him, but the lines on his face did not lighten.

"I don't believe you," he said gently. "You dove perfectly. Why would you give it up?"

"Because it's not worth the risk of crippling myself," she said, her voice urgent. "I didn't believe that a few months ago, but I believe it now. You can throw me off the Sundance, but you can't change this simple truth: I will never again enter a diving competition. That part of my life is over." She covered Reever's mouth quickly, as he had once covered hers. "No, let me finish. Diving was my way of finding a home. I don't need that anymore. I was born for the mountains and the tall grass, the pines and the wind. The Sundance is my home."

Reever searched Tory's face for long moments while the silence stretched until she called his name softly, moving against him as she whispered her love again and again. He shuddered and stilled the aching words with a kiss.

"You're wrong," Reever said finally, lifting his head until he could see Tory's eyes. "You were born for me, not the Sundance." Slowly he merged his body with hers, taking her even as he gave himself completely to her. He brought his lips to hers, worshipped her mouth, and said, "Just as I was born for you. I love you, Tory. I've loved you all my life and didn't even know it."

His whispers became hers, two voices joined in promises of love, two people discovering the beauty that would always be within their reach, a lifetime of love unfolding before them.

*   *   *   *   *

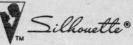

INTIMATE MOMENTS®
™ Silhouette

Ever since the appearance of Linda Howard's incredibly popular MACKENZIE'S MOUNTAIN in 1989, we've received literally hundreds of letters, all asking that same question. At last the book we've all been waiting for is here.

In September, look for MACKENZIE'S MISSION (Intimate Moments #445), Joe's story as only Linda Howard could tell it.

And Joe is only the first of an exciting breed here at Silhouette Intimate Moments. Starting in September, we'll be bringing you one title every month in our new **American Heroes** program. In addition to Linda Howard, the **American Heroes** lineup will be written by such stars as Kathleen Eagle, Kathleen Korbel, Patricia Gardner Evans, Marilyn Pappano, Heather Graham Pozzessere and more. Don't miss a single one!

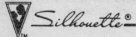

SILHOUETTE® _Desire_™ MAN OF THE MONTH

YOU'VE ASKED FOR IT, YOU'VE GOT IT!
MAN OF THE MONTH: 1992

ONLY FROM SILHOUETTE DESIRE

You just couldn't get enough of them, those men from Silhouette Desire—twelve sinfully sexy, delightfully devilish heroes. Some will make you sweat, some will make you sigh... but every long, lean one of them will have you swooning. So here they are, _more_ of the men we couldn't resist bringing to you for one more year....

BEST MAN FOR THE JOB
by Dixie Browning in June

MIDNIGHT RIDER
by Cait London in July

CONVENIENT HUSBAND
by Joan Hohl in August

NAVARRONE
by Helen R. Myers in September

A MAN OF HONOR
by Paula Detmer Riggs in October

BLUE SKY GUY
by Carole Buck in November

IT HAD TO BE YOU
by Jennifer Greene in December

Don't let these men get away! MAN OF THE MONTH, only in Silhouette Desire!

MOM92JD

TAKE A WALK ON THE DARK SIDE OF LOVE

October is the shivery season, when chill winds blow and shadows walk the night. Come along with us into a haunting world where love and danger go hand in hand, where passions will thrill you and dangers will chill you. Come with us to

In this newest short story collection from Silhouette Books, three of your favorite authors tell tales just perfect for a spooky autumn night. Let Anne Stuart introduce you to "The Monster in the Closet," Helen R. Myers bewitch you with "Seawitch," and Heather Graham Pozzessere entice you with "Wilde Imaginings."

Silhouette Shadows™
Haunting a store near you this October.

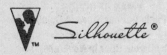